"What first   fact
that you v   war
wound," I   Most
women I meet   their
soft white hands."

Cathleen gave a low laugh. "Then you needn't worry. I have no soft white hands. If the truth be known, I'm far more accustomed to mucking out stables than pouring tea in a drawing room."

He captured her hands and held them. "Don't be ashamed of such hands. Why do you think I fell in love with you almost at first sight, except that you were wholly unlike all the women I've known?"

"Because of my ruined hands," Cathleen joked. Then his words penetrated, and her face went deathly pale. "*What* did you say?"

But Cathleen knew perfectly well what Lord Simon had just said. The question is: What *should* she . . . what *could* she . . . what *would* she . . . do?

DAWN LINDSEY was born and grew up in Oklahoma, where her ancestors were early pioneers. After graduating from college, she pursued several careers (including zoo public relations) before writing her first romance novel. She is the winner of the 1987 Romantic Times Reviewers Choice Award for Best Regency Romance for *The Great Lady Tony.* She and her attorney husband now make their home in the San Francisco area.

Dunraven's Folly

Dawn Lindsey

A SIGNET BOOK

NEW AMERICAN LIBRARY

A DIVISION OF PENGUIN BOOKS USA INC.

NAL BOOKS ARE AVAILABLE AT QUANTITY DISCOUNTS WHEN USED TO
PROMOTE PRODUCTS OR SERVICES. FOR INFORMATION PLEASE WRITE
TO PREMIUM MARKETING DIVISION, NEW AMERICAN LIBRARY,
1633 BROADWAY, NEW YORK NEW YORK 10019.

SIGNET TRADEMARK REG. U.S.PAT. OFF. AND FOREIGN COUNTRIES
REGISTERED TRADEMARK—MARCA REGISTRADA
HECHO EN DRESDEN, TN., U.S.A.

SIGNET, SIGNET CLASSIC, MENTOR, ONYX, PLUME, MERIDIAN and NAL
BOOKS are published by New American Library, a division of Penguin Books USA
Inc., 1633 Broadway, New York, New York 10019

First Printing, December, 1989

1 2 3 4 5 6 7 8 9

PRINTED IN THE UNITED STATES OF AMERICA

1

"Hell and the devil confound it!"

Major Lord Simon Grey, late of His Majesty's Ninety-fifth Rifle Battalion, feelingly took in the unmistakable signs of neglect all around him, a telltale cleft between his fair brows and the new deep lines of pain carved even more deeply than usual in his lean cheeks.

Even to his inexperienced eye it was obvious that Dunraven Downs was not the prosperous racing stable he had been led to expect. The grass was overgrown and choked with weeds, the fences sagging and in need of a fresh coat of paint. Nor was there anyone around at an hour when the place should have been bustling with grooms and horses and exercise boys. On a chilly, overcast March morning with a hint of late frost in the air, the whole aspect was frankly depressing.

And since the major had been warned by a number of friends not to hire Sir James Dunraven to train his newly acquired racehorse, he knew himself to be suffering from all the natural annoyance of a man who might even at that moment have been snug and warm in London, but for his own stubbornness.

The groom seated passively beside him cast him a brief worried look, but wisely said nothing.

But as if aware of this scrutiny, the major added frankly, "And you needn't bother reminding me, Bob! I am painfully aware that we have been jolted over indifferent roads for the better part of two days and endured a sleepless night in an inferior inn, all for the sake of my damnable temper."

The groom, a weather-beaten, rather nondescript-looking man, betrayed a hint of a grin in his somber eyes. "Aye, but then, when did that ever stop your lordship, I'd like to know?" he inquired quizzically. "Seems to me I remember many's the time you dragged the whole troop of us over impossible terrain, just to gain a half-day's advantage over the enemy."

The major laughed reluctantly. "Yes, but I fear I haven't even that excuse this time. If certain well-meaning but chuckle-headed friends hadn't tried to convince me not to undertake such an arduous journey in my present weakened condition, doubtless I'd have had the sense to send for Dunraven to wait on me in London, as I should have done."

Then he frowned again. "As it is, it was a tactical error to have come all this way, which is unlike me. It lends unpleassant weight to what I had intended to be no more than a tentative discussion. Now I'm afraid it's going to be damnably awkward to back out without an unpleasant scene."

They had reached the stable blocks by then, and the major was at least relieved to see that there were some signs of recent care. The loose boxes and near paddocks boasted a fresh coat of paint, and the cobblestoned stableyard showed signs of having been recently and ruthlessly scrubbed.

Several horses lifted their heads from their delicate cropping to regard the strangers incuriously as they passed, and a short weather-beaten man who bore the unmistakable stamp of an ex-jockey subjected them to a searching stare.

After a moment he slowly removed the pipe from his mouth and raised one hand to his cap in an ironic greeting.

"Friendly, ain't he?" remarked Aikins, the groom, his brows raised comically.

But when the major looked up again, the man was nowhere in sight.

Whether or not he had gone to warn someone, a redheaded urchin was waiting for them when they pulled up before the house, and ran to the horses' heads. He, too, regarded the newcomers with open surprise, but remarked knowledgeably, "Coo! That's a bang-up turnout, yer honor! Reg'lar sixteen-mile-an-hour tits, I reckon."

The major laughed despite himself. "If so, the credit's not mine, I fear. They belong to my brother. Is your master at home?"

"I ain't seen him go out," the lad offered cheekily. "But if it's business yer after, it's Miss Cat you'll be wanting to see."

The major wondered who Miss Cat might be. "Thank you, but I have an appointment with Sir James."

He handed the reins to Aikins, and negotiated the awkward descent to the ground, watched with unabashed interest by the youth. The major was not yet used to the curiosity he aroused, but merely shrugged and accepted his stick from the groom.

Aikins, by far less resigned to this painful scene than his master, said gruffly, "I'll see to the chestnuts meself, Major. I take it you won't be long?"

The major grinned cheerfully, perfectly well aware of the reason for his groom's sudden gruffness. "No, but in this cold you'd better rub them down and stable them. Gerry will have my hide if I let anything happen to his precious pair."

He knew that Aikins, with a reputation for efficiency

almost as good as that of Wellington's intelligence officers, could nose out far more by a casual stroll through the yard and seemingly innocuous chats with the stablehands than he himself would be able to learn in half a dozen formal meetings with Dunraven.

He had already made up his mind not to employ Dunraven, but he had spent too many years scouting out the lay of the land when it meant the difference between life and death for himself and his men to easily abandon such habits now.

He negotiated the awkward steps to the front door and was admitted, after a lengthy delay, by a slovenly housekeeper. She regarded him with frank suspicion and announced without preamble, "If it's Miss Cat ye've come to see, then it's a wasted journey ye've had."

She spoke in the broadest of Irish brogues and added complainingly, "Not to mention fetching me down from the attics with pullin' on the bell till I thought all the hounds of hell was broke loose! As for Miss Cat, she's down at the stables, as she always is, and more blame to them that's raised her to be more boy than girl is what I say!"

The major was beginning to be slightly amused despite himself at this highly original household, but managed to make the ancient harridan understand that he had an appointment with Sir James Dunraven.

She sniffed and looked even more disapproving, but grudgingly consented to conduct him to a parlor on the ground floor. She muttered all the while to herself that if Himself was expecting guests, he might have said so, seeing as how she'd chosen that very day to clean the attics, and her with the rheumatism so bad in her back it was a crime to have her climbin' up and down stairs the whole day long.

She left him in a room remarkable only for its degree of clutter and the complete absence of a fire to help ward off the March chill. The major, whose liking for the ridiculous had often been the despair of his friends in the regiment, was aware that at any other time he would have been delighted to have discovered so rich a vein of absurdity. But his aching leg and the knowledge that he had willfully let himself in for an awkward interview managed to dampen his appreciation, and he turned with a frown to regard the untidy room.

He had gladly stayed in far worse hovels in Portugal and Spain, and been extremely grateful for the shelter, but in his present mood he perversely found the room's shabbiness and general air of neglect inexcusable. If Dunraven hoped to do business with him, he was certainly going about it the wrong way.

He limped to the cold fireplace and stood staring grimly down into it, wondering if, after all, his brain could have been addled from his prolonged bout with fever. There seemed no other explanation for why he had willfully placed himself in so untenable a position.

When the major had first won a racehorse at play and decided on a whim to race it himself, Sir James Dunraven's name had cropped up almost immediately, for he had the reputation of being one of the shrewdest owners and trainers on the turf.

He also had the reputation of being something of a dark horse himself. Born in Ireland, where so many of the great racehorses seemed to come from, he had appeared in Newmarket nearly forty years ago with a magnificent racehorse in tow and exactly one hundred guineas to back him. To all inquiries he had refused to reveal how he had come by either the horse or the guineas.

However that might be, and whether, as was widely suspected, both had been come by dishonestly, the stallion had won that and many subsequent races and gone on to become something of a legend on the turf, and Dunraven's fortunes and reputation had risen with it. His origins had remained cloaked in obscurity, however, for he was alternately said to be the ne'er-do-well son of an Irish landowner and the ambitious offspring of common Irish sharecroppers.

Among the cynical, the latter version was the one more commonly believed, but Dunraven had been accepted readily enough in the undiscriminating world of the turf, where his uncanny eye for the horseflesh and his penchant for reckless wagers were all the recommendations needed. He was said to have once boasted he could pick the winners of all seven races at Newmarket on a particular day, and collected ten thousand pounds on the wager. He had also soon established a racing stud that at one time rivaled any in the kingdom, and built a house outside Newmarket where he could thumb his nose at his more genteel neighbors.

The knighthood had been a reward for unspecified services to the crown, but it was widely whispered that these "services" had had to do with the late and disgraceful scandal involving the Prince of Wales, now the Prince Regent, and charges of race-fixing. It was said that Dunraven had been instrumental in hushing the matter up and thus earned the undying gratitude of his sovereign, who even then was already growing disgusted with his eldest son's excesses.

The major, to whom all these stories had duly been repeated, had merely been amused by such extravagant tales. More than one earnest and well-meaning friend had warned him that Dunraven was an out-and-out rogue of the sort that had blackened the sport of horseracing for far too long. But the major, impatient at being tied by the heels by his slowly recovering wounds, and looking for an interest to take himself out of his gloomy thoughts, had felt a sneaking sympathy for anyone who managed to defy society's dictates. Certainly Dunraven's colorful reputation had merely aroused his curiosity.

But it seemed now that he should have paid more attention to the rumors that Dunraven had fallen on hard times of late. The major might have been noted in the regiment for his tolerance and his somewhat inconvenient sense of humor, but he drew the line when eccentricity crossed into outright pecularity. His own men had always toed the line smartly, for he knew from experience that no well-run outfit could survive without discipline.

Even so, it was annoying to think he would now have to start over. Either that or completely give up the notion of setting up his own racing stables.

The most obvious solution had always been to send the horse to Salford, his family's principal seat, where his father maintained a justly famous stud. But for several reasons the major was resolved not to do that. In the first place, he had just managed to escape from Salford's stultifying formality and his family's overanxious solicitude, and had no wish to go back. His family had never approved of his military ambitions, and his mother, for one, was transparently eager to gather him back into the fold.

That undoubtedly included marriage to one of the wealthy and well-bred heiresses she collected, and settling down to the life of a country gentleman. But such a life had never held any appeal for him and it would be doubly hard to resist her ambitions now, when he knew he was fitted for very little else.

But second, and far more important, he had an absurd desire to succeed or fail on his own, and not merely trade on his family's great name. As the younger son of the Duke of Salford, every path had been smoothed for him, and it was only in the rough-and-tumble of military life that he had begun to come into his own. He had no wish to fall back into that velvet-lined trap once again.

The problem, he acknowledged with a rueful grimace, was

that he was abysmally ignorant on the subject of the breeding or training of racehorses. Which was exactly why he had resolved to seek out an expert trainer to teach him the ropes. Like most men, in truth, he had always before considered it a rather tame sport. He much preferred ones offering more risk and excitement to the participant than merely watching someone else gallop home to victory.

But then, he had had to accept in the last months that his days of participating in violent sports himself were obviously over. It was time he found something to fill his days before he went mad with boredom.

"Hell and the devil confound it!" he said again, in no mood to cope with finding another trainer or having to admit defeat and return to Salford after all.

"Lord Simon Grey?" inquired a cool, oddly musical feminine voice from behind him.

He had not heard the door open, and turned quickly, forgetting his damnably weak leg. For a moment he thought it would go out from under him completely, pitching him ignominiously at the newcomer's feet.

And they were remarkably pretty feet too, he saw as he struggled to regain his balance. The girl—for she was little more—bore the unmistakable coloring of the true Irish beauty, which no doubt also explained the slight, attractive lilt in her voice. Her hair was as dark as a raven's wing, and she possessed a remarkably brilliant pair of eyes the exact color of sapphires. She also boasted a straight nose, a determined little chin with just a hint of an intriguing cleft in it, and an alabaster skin that reminded him of ivory or Chinese porcelain.

She obviously had not been warned about his handicap, for her eyes widened as she took in his stick and the brief awkwardness he had displayed. But she merely repeated, a slight doubt creeping into her voice, "Lord Simon Grey?"

He was somewhat annoyed that he should have appeared before this vision in such an unflattering light, and even more annoyed that it should matter to him. She was in a shabby habit that bore unmistakable signs of having been in recent close contact with horses, and still had her gloves and whip in one hand. But nothing could disguise the elegant slenderness of her figure or the quite remarkable nature of her beauty. He found himself wondering absently what the devil such a nonpareil was doing hiding her light on this run-down estate, for even with her dubious birth she would be an asset in London.

Then he remembered that the urchin and the old harridan both had spoken of a Miss Cat, who was more boy than girl and always to be found in the stables, and said with his ready charm, "Yes. And you must be . . . Miss Cat?"

She looked slightly taken aback, but her stern expression did not soften. "I'm Cathleen Dunraven, yes. Sir James is my grandfather."

He limped forward with his peculiarly attractive smile, holding out his hand. "Forgive me. I had no idea he had a granddaughter, let alone one so beautiful. How do you do?"

She made no move to take his hand. "I fear I would have done better without this interruption, for I'm very busy," she answered coolly. "I'm sorry you have had a cold and wasted journey, my lord, but I thought Sir James made it clear in his letter to you that we can take on no outside horses now."

2

The major was so astonished that for a moment he couldn't gather his scattered wits.

He had been braced to meet with a brand of friendly, even overfriendly effusiveness that he was all too familiar with. He had even cynically suspected that the sudden appearance of a comely granddaughter was yet another clever tactic designed to pressure him into an immediate commitment.

This sudden volte-face was therefore as surprising as it was intriguing, especially since he had received a highly cordial letter from Sir James only the week before, professing great willingness to meet the son of an old acquaintance.

Unfortunately, the major was given no immediate opportunity to pursue the mystery, for at that moment they were interrupted. Miss Dunraven had evidently failed to close the door properly behind her, for it was pushed open by the harridan who had admitted him.

"Ah!" she said in her rich Irish brogue, her eyes snapping with bright malice. "I'd a suspicion I'd find ye here, Miss Cat. And the more fool ye if ye've not the sense to recognize what the good Lord has cast in yer lap!"

Miss Dunraven looked furious, and answered her sharply

in a language the major didn't recognize, but belatedly realized must be Gaelic.

As if taking that for permission, the old woman launched into a voluble tirade in the same language, in which complaint and scolding seemed to bear equal weight.

Miss Dunraven endured it impatiently for a moment or two, then interrupted by hurling a sharp question. The crone chuckled and made some retort, then added in English for the major's benefit, "And didn't the foine gent'man tell me that Himself was expectin' him? And me half-dead wi' the rheumatism in me back so it's an agony to go up and down them stairs, while that divil Patch lounges at 'is ease in some public house or another, I've no doubt."

"Oh, the divil fly away wi' ye, Brigid O'Shaughnessy!" exclaimed Miss Dunraven in exasperation. "Get back to your work!"

She then turned back to the major, her color becomingly high and her brilliant eyes flashing with temper, and said curtly, "I'm sorry, but I must go. I've wasted enough time already. You might try Sam Waters in town. He's little enough sense, but he's more honest than most and at least won't cheat you too much. Good-bye."

The major might already have made up his mind that Dunraven was the last person he wanted to train his horse, but he wouldn't have been human if he had accepted the unexpected dismissal so easily. "If you don't mind, I think I would prefer to speak to Sir James," he said pleasantly. "I've come all the way from London at his express invitation, after all."

That topped her, at least for the moment. "Are you saying Sir James knew you were coming?" she demanded incredulously.

His brows rose, but he kept his temper with an effort. "Certainly. I would show you the letter, except that I foolishly neglected to bring it with me, having never suspected there would be any need to prove my word. But I can assure you he expressed perfect willingness to entertain my proposition.''

He could see anger and something like bitter acceptance in her eyes, and again wondered what the devil was going on. But after a moment she merely said shortly, ''If so, I'm doubly sorry you've had a wasted journey. I'm afraid Sir James is suffering from a sudden illness that makes it impossible for him to see anyone.''

She sounded neither sorry nor sincere. In fact there was a certain triumph in her voice, and he strongly suspected that she was lying. The only question was, why?

''I see. I'm very sorry to hear it. His illness must have come on quite suddenly.''

''Yes, quite suddenly. Now, if you'll excuse me . . .''

But the major's eyes were suddenly fixed on something over her head, and an unholy amusement had come into them. ''I can only trust he will recover soon from this . . . unexpected illness,'' he observed politely.

''I doubt it. He's not young, and has been in bad health for some years. Now, if you don't mind, I—''

Then something in his face and his fixed stare must have alerted her, for she whirled with sudden suspicion.

''Now, Caity, me darlin','' remarked a rich voice behind her, carrying far more of an Irish lilt than hers did. ''Old, is it? I'm not in my dotage yet, I'll thank ye. And when was I ever too unwell to meet the son of an old friend?''

The major regretted that he could no longer see Miss Dunraven's face, but her figure went betrayingly rigid. ''And when did you have the sense to take care of yourself?'' she flashed back bitterly. ''At any rate, I thought we'd agreed you were going to decline Lord Simon's very obliging offer?''

There was a curious emphasis to her words, but Sir James seemed merely amused by so absurd a situation. "Ah, did we?" he remarked blandly. "But then I got to thinkin', ye know, and I said to meself: Jamie, I said, it's hard-hearted ye are indeed to be turnin' away the son of so very old an acquaintance when he's come to you for a favor."

"And what answer did you give yourself?" she demanded angrily.

The major was looking between them with considerable amusement. The quarrel, whatever it was, was obviously an old one, and he found he would have given a good deal to know what it was all about.

Then Miss Dunraven, as if bitterly recognizing defeat, flushed and turned furiously back, and it became easy to detect the resemblance between them. Sir James's hair was white and his blue eyes were faded now, though they still showed an engaging twinkle. But they were both much of a height, and the pure, furious profile Miss Dunraven had turned angrily toward them was very like her grandfather's.

In fact, seeing that profile, the major suddenly found it difficult to credit the rumors that Dunraven was no more than an Irish sharecropper's son. There were pride and breeding stamped in every line of her face and erect carriage.

But the battle, whatever it had been about, was clearly over. Dunraven came on into the room, saying jovially, his Irish accent much less in evidence now. "Lord Simon! How delightful to see you, and how ill-mannered of me to have kept ye waiting." Again his eyes twinkled engagingly at his granddaughter, as if enjoying the jest at her expense.

"*Major* Grey!" interrupted Miss Dunraven with bitter emphasis. Again it sounded oddly like a warning.

If so, Sir James blithely ignored it. "Yes, I'd heard about your injury, my boy. Bad luck. But then, such things happen." He frowned, and added in an excess of sudden ill humor, "I must apologize for the state of this room! It's as cold as the grave in here."

"You should have let us know Lord Simon was coming," retorted Miss Dunraven.

Sir James scowled at her, but when she merely shrugged and went to stand by one of the sofas, he recovered himself and said genially, "Ah, niver mind! Sit down, sit down, my boy. Have a spot of whiskey. That'll warm you better than any fire. Caitlin, fetch us both a drop, there's a good lass. You met my granddaughter, Cathleen, Lord Simon? The spit of her grandmother, she is, down to the shrew's own temper, I fear."

"Yes, we introduced ourselves," said the major in some amusement. "But if you've been ill, sir, I won't keep you."

"Nonsense! Nonsense, my boy. After all, you've come all this way to discuss business with me."

The major resigned himself, wishing he'd had the sense to go when he had the chance. He saw that his host wore his age well, but there was a betraying tremor in his hands and a slight unsteadiness of step that he could not quite disguise. There was also an unmistakable stamp of dissolution about his face that spoke of many years of hard living. But unlike his granddaughter, Sir James used his considerable charm deliberately, turning it on and off at will.

He settled himself now in a shabby armchair and waved the major to do the same. He was certainly far too downy an old bird to make the mistake of plunging immediately into the business at hand, and so chatted amiably for several moments about mutual acquaintances and inquiring after his grace, whom he said he had not had the felicity of seeing in Newmarket for some months.

"No, my . . . rather dramatic return somewhat upset everyone, I fear. But he certainly means to enter his colors in the Derby as usual, I understand."

"Ah! Ah! I've heard of that new colt of his. Promising, is he?"

"I don't know, sir," answered the major truthfully.

"Ah, well! Which reminds me, I did have the honor of seeing your brother, Lord Denbigh, in Newmarket recently. In fact, he was intent on buying a handsome pair of chestnuts, as I recall. And overpaying handsomely for the privilege, I might add," Sir James added with his engaging twinkle.

The major laughed. "If so, I beg you won't tell him so, sir. It says much for his affection for me that I'm driving them at the moment, for they're his newest pride and joy."

He smiled and thanked Miss Dunraven for the glass of whiskey she handed him, but received nothing more than a sulky glare for his pains.

But Sir James remained determinedly oblivious of any awkward undercurrents in the meeting. "Ah, yes. So my man tells me," he admitted. "Not a bad pair, even though he might have had them for half the asking price. Tell him to come to me next time he's in the market for a good bargain."

After five minutes in his company, the major was ready to believe Sir James made it his business to know everything that went on in Newmarket before anyone else did. He was well-acquainted with such types, who made their living off their very real charm and inside information, judiciously gained and even more judiciously dispensed.

He held no particular brief for or against such men, for they could be useful on occasion. But Miss Dunraven notwithstanding, the major was more convinced than ever that Sir James wasn't the right man for him. He might have gone into the sport on a whim, but he had every intention of running his own show, and he knew that with Dunraven that would be impossible.

Still, he chatted on easily, leaving it to Sir James to come to the point himself. And at long last the conversation was delicately brought round to the topic at hand. "But it's sorry I was to hear ye've had to sell out, my boy," Sir James said genially. "Mentioned in the dispatches after Ciudad Rodrigo, so I hear. But then I've always said war and the turf are the only two places left where an ambitious man can still get ahead in this world."

The major was aware he received a sudden sharp glance from Miss Cathleen Dunraven, maintaining a disapproving silence in one corner of the room. He wondered at it, but was far too experienced to attempt an answer to her grandfather's blatant flattery, and so said nothing.

"And now you think you want to go into the business of breeding and racing horses, eh?" pursued Sir James. "Well, it's an interestin' sport, I grant you. None more so if ye've a liking for the unusual, and the nerve to take it. But then, I daresay that after chasin' Boney's soldiers across half of Europe, you're thinkin' it likely to be tame by comparison. Don't you believe it, me boy! There's enough danger and risk to suit any man. And I should know."

"You surprise me, sir." The major was trying to ease his aching leg, and wondering how he might bring this highly unusual interview to a close. He had admittedly been curious at first, but after twenty minutes of the old man's company he was beginning to think longingly of a warm fire and a good meal.

Sir James chuckled. "Ah, I can see ye're thinking me a blathering old fool," he said, as if divining the major's polite, if unrevealing expression. "But I tell ye frankly that if ye're looking for something to occupy your mind and distract ye from your own worries, ye couldn't have hit upon anything more to the purpose. The turf has been my mistress now for more years than you've been alive, me lad, and I couldn't ask for a better. But then, it depends on what you mean to give to it in return. If ye mean to ge a gentleman owner and leave all the work and fun to others, ye'll find it tame enough, I warrant. But if not, ye won't be sorry.''

''I think you're forgetting that Lord Simon *is* a gentleman,'' put in Miss Dunraven unexpectedly, in a scathing voice.

The old man chuckled, in no way discomfited by her rudeness. ''I fear my Caity is a born cynic. Pay no heed to her. The point is, are you passionately interested in the sport, or merely looking for a brief distraction? Because if the latter, I'd be the first to tell ye to take a more conventional mistress. A woman'll only cheat you, not break your heart as well in the bargain, as the turf is likely to do.''

''You should know!'' said Miss Dunraven. She looked the major over almost contemptuously, and added, ''And what does Lord Simon know about horse racing? Aside from having attended a few races, I mean?''

The major was a little annoyed despite himself. ''Unfortunately, Miss Dunraven, I know very little, as you seem to surmise. Which is why I am attempting to hire someone to teach me what I don't know.''

She shrugged, unimpressed. ''You mean until you grow bored with it or find something else that takes your fancy. The turf is littered with men like you, my lord, who take a whim to racehorses and then find it far less exciting and more demanding than they had imagined. It would be better if you sent your horse to your father's stables and be done with it. That way, when you lose interest, as you inevitably will, it won't involve other people who take the sport more seriously than you do.''

The major found himself flushing, and wondered what he had done to earn so much contempt. But again Sir James merely chuckled. ''Pay no attention to Caity here, lad! She has the wasp's own tongue, that one. But she's right in one thing, at least. If ye're to succeed in the hard world of the turf, you've to give it your whole concentration. It can't remain just a hobby. Oh, there are gentleman owners, such as your respected father, and well-regarded ones too. But I'm telling you, they miss half the fun.''

He looked up and added with unexpected shrewdness, ''And I'm thinking ye're looking for just such an outlet, if you don't mind my saying so. And if I'm right, then I can say without false modesty that you'd have to go far to find anyone who can teach you more than I can. Always supposing I choose to impart my knowledge, that is.''

Miss Dunraven made an undignified noise that sounded perilously like a snort, and abruptly stalked out.

Sir James seemed wholly unembarrassed by his grand-daughter's unusual behavior. ''She's a fine lass, you understand, but headstrong,'' he confided, pouring himself out another glass of whiskey. ''Niver been broke to bridle, more's the pity. But she'll give some lucky man a proper run for his money, that I will say. But enough of this shilly-shallying. I can see ye're a straightforward man, Lord Simon, and I'm the same. And I think you wouldn't have come all this way if you weren't serious about the sport. Your soldiering days are over, and now ye're looking about you for something to fill the void, for I suspect ye'll not be content to join all the other idle young fools o' your class, wi' too much money and not enough sense. And if so, then I'm your man.''

The major was perfectly aware by then that he was being handled by an expert. But Sir James was hardly the first plausible rogue who had tried to back him into a corner. He was perfectly capable of standing up right now and politely but firmly bringing the interview to a close, without either committing himself or creating any undue unpleasantness.

In fact that was what he had had every intention of doing for the last half hour, for he had a constitutional dislike of being so shamelessly manipulated and an even greater dislike of allowing himself to be outgunned, even by such an obvious expert.

But he was not quite sure which of them, Sir James or his granddaughter, was doing the most manipulating. Was Miss Dunraven really trying to drive him away, as it appeared, or could the pair of them be playing a far deeper game, working in concert to arouse his curiosity? By now he would put nothing past so wily an old rogue.

But if that were indeed the scheme, he was forced to concede that it was a clever one. Miss Dunraven had managed to intrigue him in a way he had not been intrigued in a long time. Worse, she had struck a reluctant spark, for there was just enough truth in her accusations to rankle. He had undertaken racing on a whim, and could hardly be said to have given it much thought.

In fact, he discovered he was not quite ready to abandon the curious puzzle she had set him. And certainly for one grown heartily sick of the queue of attentive damsels always surrounding him in London, eager to cosset him and offer gentle sympathy, her acerbic treatment made for a bracing change.

He was therefore not particularly surprised to hear himself saying calmly, ''Then if we can come to terms, I agree. I have only one stipulation, and that's that since I am indeed interested in learning all I can about the sport, I reserve the right to observe your methods whenever I choose. Naturally I promise to get in your way as little as possible, and yours will always be the final word. I am perfectly aware that there can be only one company commander at a time.''

Sir James waved this aside as being unimportant, and insisted upon having another drink to toast the new partnership before getting down to any serious discussions.

Whether he was just being friendly or was indeed trying to cloud the major's brain, as the latter strongly suspected, Sir James proved to be a shrewd bargainer once they finally got down to details. It was also clear he had written his guest off, as his granddaughter so obviously had done, as a noble dilettante.

The major therefore took great satisfaction in disabusing his mind of that particular misconception, at least. He refused on principle to accede to Sir James's first terms, and made a number of demands that he cared very little about, merely to make a point. He knew that if he ever allowed Sir James to gain the upper hand, he would live to regret it.

Nor was he surprised when Sir James, once they had at last reached agreement, betrayed no rancor at the hard bargaining. "I can see we're going to hit it off well, me boy. I like a man who's not afraid to bargain. Niver trust anyone who won't hold out for his own interests, is my motto."

He insisted the major stay to dinner, but the major declined this invitation and rose with some difficulty, cursing the cold and the inevitable stiffness which made his leg almost useless after he had sat for any length of time. "Thank you, but I fear I must get back to London. You'll be hearing from me by the end of the week. I'll make arrangements to have my horse brought up as soon as possible, and let you know when to expect it."

To his mild regret he did not see Miss Dunraven again.

Once back on the road to Newmarket he received his groom's report with interest.

'It's a hem set-out, all right, Major!" said Aikins, spitting neatly over the side of the curricle. "And mighty closemouthed too, seemingly. I was kept under close escort, as you might say, by the head groom, name of Chicklade. He was polite enough, but far from being friendly, if you know what I mean. In fact, in the end I began to wonder who was pumping whom, for he was mighty full of questions about your lordship and your intentions. It was him, by the way, we saw earlier in the yard.''

"Yes, I had already suspected as much. He certainly warned someone, but whether it was Sir James or his grand-daughter, I couldn't tell. What did you think of general conditions?''

Aikins regarded him curiously, but merely shrugged. "The place has certainly come on hard times, as we'd already guessed. Only one or two undergrooms, at least on view, which is not enough to run a place that size. But then, there seem to be precious few horses about, come to that. This Chicklade seemed competent enough. I poked my nose in as many corners as I could without being too conspicuous, and things seemed well-enough-run, from the outside, at least. By the way, there was another fellow hanging about the yard—a smooth Irishman name of Patch that I wouldn't trust as far as I could throw him. But then, perhaps I'm prejudiced. I never had any liking for oily-tongued rascals myself.''

The major made no answer, and they drove on in thought-ful silence for some moments. At last Aikins added, with a sidelong glance at the major's preoccupied face, "Why the curiosity, if you don't mind my asking, Major? I thought you'd already decided the place wouldn't do.''

The major abruptly came out of his abstraction. "I did, and it won't. Nevertheless, I agreed to send the bay there as soon as possible.''

Aikins was by far too familiar with his superior officer's vagaries and somewhat inconvenient sense of curiosity to betray any surprise at this news. "Aye, I'd suspicioned as much by the questions,'' he said gloomily. "Just let you once get a whiff of a mystery, my lord, and it seems you can't rest until you've untangled it.''

The major laughed, looking suddenly more like himself than he had in months. "You know I've been looking for something to put an end to my confounded boredom. And I've a strong hunch I've just found it."

3

"Have you gone *mad?*" demanded a furious Cathleen Dunraven of her grandfather sometime later. "Chicklade tells me you've not only agreed to train Lord Simon's horse but also given him leave to wander about the place at will."

Sir James seemed in no way put off by this highly unfilial form of address. "Me that has gone mad, is it?" he countered in righteous indignation. "Who is it, I'd like to know, who showed herself in polite company stinkin' o' the stables and screechin' like a vulgar Irish fishwife, until I was fair ashamed to own ye? I can only thank God your mother, bless her saintly soul, isn't alive to see what I've let ye become."

"You can leave my mother out of this!" Cat snapped. "As for stinking of the stables or screeching like a vulgar Irish fishwife, God knows I come by both naturally. And don't try to change the subject. You deliberately led me to think you'd written to put Lord Simon off."

As always when on the ropes, Sir James took refuge in his ready anger. "I'll thank you to remember you're not mistress here yet, missy! Not by a long chalk," he roared. "It's a fine thing when a man's granddaughter thinks to question him in his own home."

"And it's a fine thing when a man stoops to playing shabby

tricks on his own granddaughter. And don't think to put me off with any of your Irish blarney! Don't forget, I know all your tricks. What the devil are you up to?''

"Aye, now that's fine, respectful talk to your grandda'. And mind your language. I'll not have ye swearin' about the place like a stablehand. Ye've the divil's own tongue between your teeth, and that's the God's truth.''

"If I have, I come by that honestly as well. I warn you, I don't trust you an inch!''

He looked rather more pleased than otherwise at this wholesale indictment, but abruptly changed tactics and began to wheedle. "It seems there's no pleasing you, Caity, me darlin'. And I suppose ye haven't been naggin' me for months past about money? But do I get any credit when I try to do something about it? At any rate I never knew ye to look askance at five hundred guineas before.''

"Aye, you may well stare,'' he added, satisfied with the reaction he had achieved. "Did ye think I'd risk your plans for a mere pittance? And there's more where that come from, I'm thinkin'. Lord Simon's a very downy pigeon an' he's fallen right into our laps. I tell you it was tempting fate to pass it up. Ye couldn't expect one to do it.''

But she knew instinctively he was up to something more than the five hundred guineas, incredible a sum as that was. "I don't care if it's five thousand,'' she said hardly. "You know the last thing we need right now is someone running tame about the place.''

He chuckled. "If that's all that's worrying ye, he'll soon tire of that. In a week he'll be longin' for the sight of London again. Show him a few training sessions, rouse him at dawn—take the glamour off the sport, so to speak—and he'll soon enough be trotting gratefully home again. Surely you can keep an eye on him that long?''

She considered it unwillingly, strongly tempted despite

herself. The sum Sir James mentioned was outrageous, and would undoubtedly come in handy in a place that seemed to run through money as if it were water. But then again her resolve hardened. "Possibly—if he weren't the son of one of the most influential owners on the turf. I tell you, it's too dangerous."

"Now, Caity, it's not like you to lose your nerve. There's little enough danger. You saw him for yourself! He's exactly the sort of sleepy young fool I'd expected, and crippled to boot. And I guarantee his money's as good as anyone else's, and better than most. I'm thinkin' ye should have little enough objection if I part him from some of it."

As usual, she marveled at his frequent blindness where anyone else was concerned. She had not thought Major Lord Simon Grey any kind of a fool, but she had no intention of saying so unless pressed. "You can part him from as much as you like," she said, "but not at the risk of ruining everything else. Nor do we have the staff to take on any more horses now. We've let people go till we've scarcely enough to keep the place going as it is."

"Ah, but with five hundred golden guineas from his lordship's purse, we'll be able to afford more. Surely ye've thought of that, and you usually so canny?"

"Aye, I'm at least canny enough to know it's difficult enough keeping our nearest neighbor from poking his long nose around whenever he chooses, without importing one of his spies ourselves and paying for the privilege?"

But as usual when their neighbor was mentioned, Sir James lost his temper. "Don't talk to me of that spalpeen Baggett, for we both know who encourages him to haunt the place, curse him for the ill-bred scroundrel he is. And I tell ye now to your face, my girl, if ye're thinkin' of wedding that oily double dealer, ye're no granddaughter of mine!"

"I'll marry whom I please," she retorted, unimpressed.

"And if you don't want Baggett hanging about, then you shouldn't have pledged the Downs to him on the back of a spavined nag."

For a moment he looked near to apoplexy. Then abruptly he burst out laughing. "Aye, it's your mother's own tongue ye have in your head, girl," he said in unwilling admiration. "But let me hear no more talk of spavined nags. Ye know as well as I do that that race wasn't honestly run, curse Baggett's black English heart. He's a disgrace to the sport, so he is, and it was a black day when he decided to ape his betters by setting up as gentleman-owner."

"It was an even blacker one when you gave him a note on the Downs we can't afford to redeem. And when you agreed to allow a stranger leave to wander around here at will at a time when we have everything to hide," she said, returning to the subject at hand. "You're up to something, damn you, and I intend to find out exactly what it is."

Again he looked pleased. "Oh, you do, do ye? Well, I'll tell you, ye're a good girl and a beautiful blue-eyed witch when it comes to the sweet-talkin' of horses. But ye're no match for me, my girl, and niver will be. And as for Baggett, I've me eyes on a way to pay him back in full, never ye fear. *And* redeem my notes-of-hand, curse him for the black-hearted blackguard he is. I may be old, but I've still one or two tricks up me sleeve, I'm thinkin'."

"You'll have one or two tricks up your sleeve when St. Peter meets you at the pearly gates," she replied bitterly. "But I warn you, if they have anything to do with Lord Simon Grey, he's not the fool you think him."

He eyed her with his sudden and always unwelcome shrewdness. "What's this? Have ye taken an unexpected liking to his lordship lass?"

She flushed and then cursed the betraying sign. For that reason she made her voice even harder than usual. "I'm simply telling you he's no pigeon for your plucking, however much you may have gulled him into paying you for the doubtful privilege of having his horse trained here. I don't trust him. He didn't like anything he saw here, and had every intention of telling you to go to the devil. I know he did. The point is, why didn't he?''

But she might have spared her breath. Sir James's vanity was far too great for him ever to credit anyone else with even a spark of his own abilities. ''It might be because he knows there's no one else who can give him a winner. Have you thought of that, by any chance? You do me less than credit, lass. I tell you, the day's not dawned yet when even so canny a bird isn't ripe for my plucking. He's a fledgling, a green young fool, an impudent puppy if he thinks to match wits with a genius of my caliber.''

For once she was not even even tempted to smile at his colossal vanity. ''He's also a major in the Ninety-fifth Rifles,'' she said deliberately. ''Did you know that? Jamie will tell you they're not noted for having green young fools as officers.''

''And how would ye be finding that out, I'm wondering?'' Sir James demanded thoughtfully.

Again she flushed, and was annoyed with herself. ''Chicklade managed to get it out of his groom. And whether or not I'm right, he's still the younger son of the Duke of Salford. Too much is at stake to risk everything now.''

He was still eyeing her curiously, but he waved that aside as unimportant. ''It's unlike ye to lose your nerve, lass. Ye've usually the coolest head I know.''

She looked suddenly immensely weary. ''Have I? I think sometimes that I'd almost be relieved to see the Downs go, and be done with it.''

But this heresy was too much for him. ''What the divil's got into ye this morning? Ye've racin' in your blood, the same as it's in mine, and your father's and Jamie's. It's the one heritage ye'll never escape from. Ye should know that by now.''

"Perhaps. But it's not in Jamie's blood, however much you'd like to think it is." She was suddenly in deadly earnest. "Let him go, Grandfather. He's not like us. He hates it all, the lying and the trickery. Let him join the army and escape before it's too late."

But he was once more unreachable, safe behind his impenetrable shield of optimism. "Jamie's a weakling!" he said scathingly. "Ye're twice the man he is, and always will be."

She laughed without humor. "Am I? Has it never occurred to you that that's hardly an ambition for one of my sex? Oh, never mind! At any rate, all that's beside the point. Write and put his lordship off, before it's too late. He can easily find another trainer."

But she knew she might as well have spared her breath. Sir James had always been a law unto himself. It was useless to expect him to see anything outside his own colossal self-confidence.

Nor could she begin to explain, even to herself, why Major Lord Simon Grey, with his upright military bearing and charming smile, had somehow aroused all her hackles immediately, as a rabbit will instinctively react to a danger it senses but cannot understand.

She had expected, if she had bothered to give the matter any thought, that he would be like all the other overbred young fools who haunted Newmarket, with too much money to spend and the absolute conviction that the world owed them special privileges because of their august birth.

In fact, when he had first written to tell Sir James that he had won a horse at play and decided on a whim to set up his own racing colors, she had had little doubt he would represent everything she most despised in the sport of racing: the wealthy and disinterested owners who thought to pay others to take over all the drudgery and heartbreak for them while they smilingly accepted the prizes and compliments for other people's work.

She had convinced Sir James, not without difficulty, to refuse the offer—or so she had thought. When Chicklade had come to warn her of his lordship's arrival that afternoon, she had merely thought it a belated attempt to convince Sir James to change his mind.

But she should have known her grandfather was up to no good. It was unlike him to give in so easily once his mind was made up.

Nor had she expected Lord Simon Grey, far from being the Sprig of Fashion she had been expecting, to turn out to possess a firm, attractive countenance and a decided air of command—not to mention a pair of laughing gray eyes that seemed to invite one to share in the jest. He had been surprisingly tall and broad-shouldered, but much too thin, and it was easy to see he had recently been very ill.

He had also obviously been enduring a good deal of pain from his stiff leg, if the faint frown between his eyes and the new, deep lines in that weather-hardened face were anything to go by. But she had certainly not expected the cheerful unconcern with which he did so, nor the surprising shock of fair hair bleached to gold by the sun that made him look endearingly boyish.

In short, he had looked nothing like what she had expected, and she had had to resist a foolish and wholly uncharacteristic urge to smooth away those lines between his fair brows.

But no one knew better than she how dangerous such feelings were. She had instantly hardened her heart and treated him with deliberate rudeness. But not only had he held on to his temper with remarkable good humor; she could not quite dismiss the highly galling suspicion that he had secretly been laughing at her the whole time.

Certainly he had been indulging his obviously over-developed sense of humor at her expense when Sir James had entered the room to complete making her look an utter fool.

Oh, the devil with them both! The truth was, Lord Simon Grey possessed that brand of quiet good breeding and self-confidence that never failed to make her feel furiously inferior, and that was all it was.

She could have borne that, of course, for they were unlikely to see much of one another—at least if she had anything to do with it. But he also appeared to be exactly the sort of shrewd, straightforward man they had most reason to fear at the moment. And unlike her grandfather, she had never relished playing with fire for the sheer risk of being burned.

The thought stiffened her resolve, and she turned back, her face hard. "You know I've never interfered in your schemes before. In fact, I've told you you may take him for any amount you care to, so long as it doesn't threaten my plans. But I warn you, I won't stand by and watch you ruin everything for the sake of a few hundred pounds."

"And I'll remind you I'm still above ground! And as long as that's so, *I'm* still master here, my girl! If ye think to cross swords with me, ye're even more of a fool than I thought ye! Now, I've given Lord Simon my word, and that's final! If ye've any complaints, then go and marry Baggett and be damned to ye!"

Cat hesitated as he stormed out, then gave it up as futile and let him go. She had little doubt that he had deliberately whipped himself into a fury in an effort to put an end to an argument in which he felt himself to be on shaky ground. But she also knew from bitter experience that if she persisted, he would merely take refuge in a sudden onslaught of decrepitude and retire to his bed with none but the disgraceful Patch allowed near. Only when he thought the subject safely forgotten would he emerge again, his health miraculously restored.

In fact, Sir James was as slippery as he was exasperating, so she had given up trying to get the better of him.

But she was not his granddaughter for nothing. And there was more than one way to get rid of Lord Simon Grey. She had long since jettisoned any scruples she might have possessed, and she would not see all her hopes carelessly ruined by a charming nobleman looking for momentary amusement.

Not even for a war hero with a surprisingly likable face and laughing gray eyes.

4

Major Lord Simon Grey, in the meantime, was ruefully aware that he had foolishly allowed his curiosity to overcome his better judgment. A mere strong desire to discover what was behind Miss Cathleen Dunraven's highly unusual behavior did not now seem explanation enough for committing himself to such an unwise arrangement.

In fact, he was tempted even yet to back out. But he had give his word, and so made the necessary arrangements to have the bay delivered to Dunraven.

He was conscious as he did so of a surprisingly strong inclination to accompany the horse. He resisted it, knowing his desire had far more to do with an inexplicable urge to see Miss Cathleen Dunraven again than with any compulsion to ensure the well-being of so valuable an animal. Nor could he explain, even to himself, why his interest should have been so fairly caught by a sulky Irish beauty with execrable manners and a wily old rogue for a grandfather. Especially when he had been resisting the lures of far more conciliating London damsels for weeks now.

But then, perhaps that had a great deal to do with it. He knew himself to be still overly sensitive about his handicap, and frequently found it hard to bear the well-meaning sympathy of his friends and acquaintances. Fashionable young ladies, in particular, seemed to vie with each other to fetch stools for his injured leg or pillows for his back, and frequently insisted upon rejecting eligible partners for the dubious privilege of sitting out a pair of dances with him.

No doubt he should have been flattered by such attention, but he was not vain enough to think it had anything to do with him. He was certainly too modest to realize that his campaign-hardened body and the air of command that sat so easily on him, when allied with his attractive, pain-tautened countenance, tended to make the usual fashionable young gentleman-about-town appear pale and uninteresting by comparison.

But if the major was blind to the particular source of his attraction, his rivals were by no means so shortsighted. More than one young pink had found himself in the unusual position of passionately wishing that he himself possessed so interesting a limp, and could thus impress everyone with the nobility of his suffering.

Of course, in reality it would be dashed inconvenient not to be able to dance, or ride to hounds, or any of the dozens of things that kept a fellow from dying of boredom. And in point of fact Lord Simon was a damned good fellow, and one it was impossible not to like. But still, it was a shabby trick to play on his friends, and tended to make a fellow sorry he had missed the opportunity of becoming a hero himself.

The irony that he could be envied for the handicap that had so profoundly changed his own life would undoubtedly have brought a quick flash of amusement to the major's deep gray eyes, had he guessed it. He only knew that he sometimes had to stand, his lean cheeks rigid and his lips tightly folded together, until he could master his temper enough to respond with politeness to some well-meant offer of an arm or a hastily brought chair. He disliked being fussed over, and frequently offended people by his refusal to be treated as an invalid.

Which perhaps went far to explain why the surly behavior of Miss Dunraven should have appealed to him so strongly. She certainly had been surprised by his handicap, but had neither fussed over him nor betrayed any desire to accord him special privileges. In fact, she had been deliberately rude to him.

The thought that that should be the treatment he preferred made him grin, and he could almost hear the teasing of his friends back in the regiment were they to hear of it. The truth was, of course, that he was confoundedly bored. After having been tied by the heels for months, recovering from his wound and the far more unpleasant effects of the accompanying fever, he didn't seem to know what to do with himself.

He had escaped from Salford as soon as he could and gone to London, where he still had a number of friends and could find more to distract him. But he had found it very little better. Ten years of campaigning seemed to have created more of a gulf than he had expected, and he didn't seem able to pick up the threads of his old life again. He had never thought of himself as a particularly serious fellow—in fact, he had a reputation in the regiment for taking nothing serious, not even the bloodiest battle. He and the other young officers who were his friends were in the habit of cracking jokes on the most serious of subjects, and spent every minute between campaigns flirting with the local beauties, putting together makeshift hunts, and generally getting up to mischief.

But he could not seem to accustom himself to the fact that in London nothing seemed to matter but the cut of one's coat or the latest scandalous *on-dit*. Certainly the recent Regency crisis had drawn far more attention than Wellington's progress on the Peninsula.

The major tried to curb his growing impatience, but the

truth was that to one who had faced death almost daily for years, and had had the responsibility for the fate of hundreds of men on his shoulders, spending one's afternoons paying calls or betting at Tatt's, and one's evenings at an endless series of balls, ridottos, and musical evenings, soon began to pall.

Things wouldn't have been nearly so bad, of course, if he had had any outlet for his growing restless energy. But since he could neither ride nor box nor dance, nor even indulge in the mildest of strolls in the park without exhausting himself, his frustration was becoming acute. Used to almost constant physical exercise, his days spent in the saddle in all kinds of weather, followed by a bivouac in a drafty hovel if he was lucky, or a camp tent if he wasn't, he found that even as his health improved, his temper seemed to deterioriate accordingly. The luxury in which he had grown up and always taken for granted suddenly seemed shallow and unnecessary, and the accoutrements of civilization stifling.

Once, when his leg had been bothering him more than usual and he hadn't been able to sleep, he had thrown his coverlet down on the floor and spent the rest of the night there, dropping off to sleep almost immediately. His valet had been profoundly shocked the next morning to almost stumble over him, and plainly had not understood the major's somewhat sheepish explanation that he was so used to catching a nap anywhere that a proper bed sometimes seemed to suffocate him.

Certainly his noble family had never understood his military ambitions, any more than they had been able to understand that he had always been grateful he had been born the younger son and thus spared the stultifying expectations that had always hedged his brother Gerry round. He had a constant need to be *doing something*, which made his present enforced inactivity all the more unbearable.

He grinned again nostalgically, thinking that military life had certainly more than satisfied that urge, at least. It had frequently been even hotter than he'd bargained for, but he had never regretted his decision. He knew without false modesty that he had been an excellent officer, and one able to inspire uncommon loyalty in his men. They knew from experience that he would never ask them to go anywhere he himself wouldn't. They were fond of saying that if Major Grey was with them they never knew what they were likely to get into. Like as not he'd risk all of their necks in some harebrained and highly dangerous scheme or other—but since he never failed to bring them out safe again, *and* more often than not with some vital piece of ground nobody thought could be taken, none of them ever held it against him.

His long-suffering friends said merely that he must have been born under a lucky star, or else had as many lives as a cat. And it did seem as if he were phenomenally lucky. He had once adopted a whole family of shepherds in the Pyrenees who were in dire straits, causing his superior officers to complain and even his men to grumble under their breaths at the inconvenience and stench of having a herd of sheep overrunning the camp and always underfoot.

But not only had the fresh mutton come in handy, as the major had easily foreseen; as luck would have it, those same shepherds had been able to guide them over a pass that cut three days off their march and allowed them to surprise the French and gain a considerable advantage. Simon's friends had all shaken their heads and said that Lucky Simon would land on his feet no matter which way you threw him. Doubtless if you dropped him in the middle of enemy lines, he'd talk his way out *and* bring home half a dozen French prisoners with him!

Unfortunately, his luck had finally run out at the bloody siege of Ciudad Rodrigo. Or, more accurately, he knew himself to be amazingly lucky to have emerged alive and reasonably whole. The army doctors had wanted to take his left leg off above the knee, predicting pessimistically that even if he managed to survive the trauma to the muscle and the loss of blood and the almost inevitable gangrene that would follow—none of which seemed likely at the moment— the leg would certainly never be of any use to him again.

But the major, more dirty and exhausted and stunned by pain and the extent of the butchery he had just taken part in than he ever wanted to be again, had known instinctively that life as only half a man was hardly worth living, and had refused to give his consent.

The doctors were too overworked and weary themselves to bother arguing with a man likely to die in the next few hours anyway. They had gloomily shaken their heads and given up on him, then hurried on to the next in the seemingly endless line of dead and dying still awaiting their attention.

And certainly, for many weeks afterward, the major was to have good reason to believe their dire prognostications had been unduly optimistic. The evacuation from the front had been an experience he did not like to dwell on. He learned later that almost as many of the wounded had succumbed to the agony of being jolted in exposed carts over execrably bad roads in the burning heat or torrential rains, and with little or no opium to blur their pain, as had died in those first hours.

He only knew that he had been more dead than alive himself, and soon racked by alternate fever and chills. If it hadn't been for Aikins, who had found him and done what he could for him, he almost certainly would have died.

By the time they reached the makeshift hospital in Lisbon, he was no longer certain that that had been a good thing. He was mostly out of his head, and so recalled little of the next few weeks. He would rouse occasionally to become aware of the heat and decay and the inescapable smell of death all around him, and Aikins' strained face, then give in gratefully to the comforting blackness sucking him back down again into welcome oblivion.

The worst had been the recurring fever-fed nightmares. He had dreamt again and again that they had taken his leg off while he slept. He would wake in gut-wrenching horror, only to be reassured by the agony in his shattered thigh and Aikins' calm voice, and so fall back into a fevered sleep again. In fact, the pain had sometimes been the only thing to cling to in that nightmare world. He had welcomed it as proof that he was still alive.

But to almost everyone's surprise, including his own, he had slowly recovered, and finally been shipped back to England. But after weeks in the overcrowded hospital and then the nightmare journey on the transport home, he had been so emaciated a skeleton that even his old nurse had scarcely recognized him.

He had built back quickly after that, under the determined care of a host of old family retainers. And despite the pessimistic predictions of the expensive doctors his family had insisted upon consulting, he had even regained the limited use of his leg. He could walk, though clumsily and only by leaning heavily on a stick, and the effort admittedly cost him considerable agony. But he was determined not to give in to the life of a permanent cripple.

Keeping depression at bay now seemed to be his chief problem. The future stretched bleakly before him, and it was sometimes difficult not to wonder bitterly if all the pain and struggle had been worth it.

He knew he was being damnably surly and ungrateful, especially to those who had sacrificed so much to keep him alive. But he could not yet reconcile himself to the constricted life of a country gentleman and marriage to one of his mama's handpicked candidates, which seemed the only fate left open to him.

Which was why, when he had won a racehorse at play, he had latched on to it almost as a drowning man would a lifeline. And why he was now having trouble resisting the temptation to be present when the horse arrived in Newmarket, in order to further his acquaintance with the mysterious and annoying Miss Cathleen Dunraven.

He successfully managed to resist the impulse for a full week, and even made several social engagements for the day he had appointed. But his long-suffering groom was not particularly surprised to find the major canceling those appointments at the last minute and accompanying the bay on the uncomfortable journey to Newmarket.

Certainly both soon began to develop a healthy respect for the difference between a horse bred for racing and those military mounts they were used to, chosen primarily for their stamina and docility. The bay was nervous and bad-tempered, and betrayed a vicious tendency to lash out at any of his handlers who made the mistake of getting within range of his flashing teeth or hooves.

He settled down a little on the road, led by a groom mounted on a horse that had been a stablemate. But he took frequent exception to other traffic, and betrayed by his twitching skin and rolling eyes that his temper was merely banked down, not calmed, and could erupt again at any moment. It was also obvious by the healthy respect his grooms showed him that they were afraid of him and would be relieved to turn him over to other hands.

Luckily the weather had improved, and it was a lovely

spring day. Even Dunraven Downs, when they arrived in the early afternoon, looked more promising with the trees beginning to leaf out and a delicate green casting a gracious canopy over its neglect.

The London grooms, however, looked unimpressed, and the major was once again aware that he was making an extremely foolish decision. He had learned enough of the bay on the trip to realize that Sir James, with his small staff and run-down operation, would have to be a miracle worker to handle such an animal.

Nor was there any sign of Sir James or his unruly granddaughter when they at last reached the stable block. They were met by the unsmiling groom the major had seen once before, and an earnest young man whom the major took, after one look, to be his son.

The only other persons in the yard were the redheaded lad also seen on the last visit, who grinned cheekily at him, and a lounging figure whose impertinent stare and obvious detachment from events seemed to indicate he expected to be entertained.

The major soon saw why. Chicklade, the groom, looked the bay over unrevealingly, but Conqueror was not nearly so reticent about his immediate dislike of his new home. He took one look at the clean stall awaiting him and flatly refused to enter it.

The London grooms grinned to themselves, but did their best to coax the bay in. When that failed, they tried to force him in, sweating and cursing and trying to remain out of reach of those vicious teeth and hooves.

Meanwhile the redheaded youth added to the confusion by dashing in and out of the fray, and the detached observer chewed on a straw and looked as if he were enjoying himself hugely.

Chicklade had remained passive, with something like

contempt on his face, and made no attempt to interfere. The major was beginning to be annoyed by that time, but could do nothing more than stand on the sidelines and fume.

He was about to call a halt to the goings-on when one of the town-bred grooms lost his temper at last and slashed brutally at the bay with his whip.

It was not a mere riding crop, but a long-handled affair of braided leather, capable of doing considerable damage. As the major started forward in anger, his weak leg momentarily forgotten, the bay screamed anew with terror and passion and rounded on his tormentors, his coat beginning to show wet patches of sweat, and foam showing at his nostrils. He was beyond control, rearing and plunging until he was in as much danger of damaging himself as the men crouching back away from him.

The major was blindly furious, as much at his own helplessness as at the stupidity of the groom. He raised his voice to order the grooms back, but it merely added to the fray. He had never felt so useless.

Then, as the groom once more raised his whip, from out of nowhere snicked the thonged end of a carriage whip. It neatly lifted the raised whip from the groom's hand and sent it flying harmlessly.

For a moment the groom seemed as astonished as the rest of them, staring at his hand as if he still expected the whip to be there.

Then Miss Cathleen Dunraven's calm, icy voice demanded from behind them, ''What the *devil* is going on here?''

5

For a moment they were all too stunned to react. The major found himself falling guiltily silent along with the rest of them, as if he had been responsible for that deplorable scene.

Miss Dunraven paid no attention to any of them. She eyed the groom who was nursing his hand in growing anger and added contemptuously, "Now, get out, and take the others with you. I won't have anyone on my property who mishandles horses."

Recovering, the groom swore and started forward, pain and fury suffusing his face. "Why, you little—"

The major found his voice at last. "*That's enough!*" he thundered. "You've had your marching orders! Now, move!"

Miss Dunraven shot Simon a scornful look, but stood her ground, betraying absolutely no fear. For a moment longer the issue seemed to hang in the balance, and the major tensed himself, uncertain what he would do if the groom refused to back down. From the corner of his eye he saw that Chicklade had also moved imperceptibly closer, and his hand had gone quietly to his pocket, though he did not withdraw it.

But the command in the major's voice, and the belated realization that he had overstepped himself, seemed to bring the groom to his senses. He stopped, and touched his hat in exaggerated deference, "Awwright, miss, if that's the way you want it. We'll be glad to go, won't we, boys? But just as a matter o' curiosity, how was you thinkin' of handling this hell-spawned brute? With this old man and a boy? Or perhaps you're expectin' his lordship here to help you, with his crippled leg? Mysel', I been with this cursed nag for more'n a year now, and nothin' but a whip ever got through to 'im. But no doubt they do things different where you come from."

His companions were grinning by now, and stepped ostentatiously back, as if washing their hands of the whole affair. Young Chicklade was flushed with anger, and the major was annoyed, both at the gibe at his helplessness and at the insulting references to her Irish birth. Only Chicklade and Miss Dunraven seemed to have remained untouched by the slighting words.

The former quietly removed his hand from his pocket and settled back as if he no longer had any need to worry, and the latter calmly threw away her whip and took a deep breath.

The younger Chicklade had managed to retain his hold on the leading rein, but he, too, grinned now, as if expecting a rare show. Earlier it had been all he could do to keep his feet on the ground under the bay's plunging, but now he relaxed and let the rein go slack.

It seemed that only the major had no idea what to expect. Miss Dunraven ignored them all, and holding out her hand, calmly began to advance on the still-terrified bay, speaking softly all the while in a musical tongue that the major by now recognized as Gaelic. All trace of her former fury was gone, nor was there any hint of fear in that proud, beautiful face.

The major made a convulsive movement as if to prevent her, but in the end could do nothing but stand back and watch as well. He was too far away to intervene, and ran the real risk of increasing her danger if he called out or tried to stop her.

Even the London grooms had stopped grinning, as if this was the last thing they had expected. The major was conscious that they all seemed to be holding their breath as she advanced slowly but steadily on the bay.

The bay, as if as startled as the men, stood backed into one corner, trembling and jerking his head restlessly. For the moment he was relatively quiet, but not one of them needed to be told that he was a powder keg likely to go off again at any moment.

Only Cathleen Dunraven betrayed no awareness of the danger. She advanced steadily, almost crooning to the horse in that soft, musical tongue. Conqueror backed nervously before her, stamping and snorting, his skin twitching with fear and temper. But for the moment, at least, he made no move to attack her. He seemed as curious as the rest of them about the foolish human who advanced so fearlessly upon him.

Slowly Cat approached, her hand held steady and her voice never faltering. The horse's trembling increased, and again he backed nervously. The major felt as if his heart had lodged permanently in his throat, but he too remained silent, as if mesmerized by this remarkable display. He didn't need to imagine what would happen to that beautiful face or slender, elegant body if the bay slashed out at her with his deadly hooves. She was far too close to evade them.

Still Cat didn't hurry. She stopped a scant two feet from the bay and stood fearlessly, her hand held out, as if waiting for the horse to make the next move. A murmur rose from the spectators, quickly hushed, as slowly the bay reached out his great head, his nostrils flaring and his eyes still rolling in fear.

The major felt his breath escape in a sudden rush of

mingled relief and incredulity as the bay at last stepped
forward and dipped his head under her hand to invite her
stroking. He looked so docile that it was hard to believe he
had terrorized five grown men only moments before.

She continued to stroke him for a minute, still crooning
to him in that soft, incomprehensible language. Then at long
last she took his bridle from the grinning young Chicklade
and led Conqueror into the stall as easily as if he had been
a child's pony.

"Well, I'll be damned!" exclaimed the leader of the
London grooms, as if for all of them.

She emerged from the stall, the halter in her hand.
"Probably!" she said satirically, and tossed the halter to
young Chicklade and walked off. The bay stuck his head over
the half-door and whinnied softly after her, as if she had
raised him from a foal.

The major was also having trouble believing the exhibition
he had just witnessed, but roused himself to order the grooms
to leave. They went willingly enough, all of the bravado
knocked out of them.

He could scarcely blame them. It was the most remarkable
display of bravery he had ever seen. In fact, he'd never before
doubted his own courage, but he was willing to admit he
would not lightly have approached an animal in that mood.
Even now the memory of what could have happened made
him shudder.

The elder Chicklade took in the major's evident bemuse-
ment with something like humor, and remarked laconically
over the lighting of his pipe, "Happen the bay'll be tractable
enough now, my lord."

"Good God, I can believe it. That's the damnedest
demonstration I've ever encountered! How the devil does
she do it?"

The groom shrugged and made sure he had his pipe going

to his satisfaction. "Himself calls it 'witchin'," he said indifferently. "It's always seemed as good an explanation as any."

"I can almost believe it *was* witchcraft. In fact, if I hadn't seen it with my own eyes, I don't think I'd have believed it. By 'Himself' I take it you mean Sir James? Can he 'witch' them too?"

Chicklade removed his pipe stem from his teeth and spat. "I've been around 'em so long, they've got me talkin' Irish half the time," he said with some disgust. "Aye, he's a rare hand with horses. But to my mind he's not got Miss Cat's touch."

"I think I'm glad there aren't two of them. It's . . . almost eerie."

"I been workin' round horses fifty years, man and boy, and I'll confess I ain't never seen anything like it," admitted the groom. "But then, Miss Cat could ride anythin' you threw her across from the time she was a passionate tot o' three."

"Yes, I remember the housekeeper called her more boy than girl. But that goes beyond either. Have you worked here long?" he added curiously.

The groom once more seemed to lapse into monosyllables. "Aye. If there's nothing else you wanted, I'd best see to the bay, my lord."

The major recognized with rueful annoyance that he had been politely but firmly dismissed. It occurred to him that Dunraven Downs was growing hourly more mysterious, with its annoying secrecy—not to mention a beautiful young woman who could witch horses, and a taciturn groom who seemed to carry a pistol in his pocket as part of his duties. The major was tempted to startle Chicklade out of his unnatural calm by questioning him about that, but after a moment merely nodded and accepted the dismissal.

"No, nothing else. I'll be back in the morning to see how the bay spent the night." He said it almost warningly, daring the groom to object, but the other said nothing. "Be good enough to inform Sir James, if you will."

The groom took some moments to knock out his pipe and restore it to his pocket. "Aye," he said at last. "But ye'll soon find it's Miss Cat who calls the shots round here, my lord. Good day to you."

As he strode off with his rolling gait, the major caught sight of the impudent observer he had noticed earlier.

The fellow, who had been blatantly listening to his conversation, turned and winked broadly before tipping his hat and laughingly sauntering away.

Aikins, who had remained in the background until now, though he had stepped quietly forward when it had looked earlier as if the major was going to be forced to intervene, growled something under his breath now. At the major's questioning gaze he pronounced disapprovingly, "If you ask me, there's queer doin's here, Major. Let alone they're all about as welcoming as a room o' French field marshals— and about as friendly!"

The major eyed him thoughtfully for a moment. "Yes. But you must admit that that was an impressive display. I'm begining to think it may not have been such a mistake to bring the bay here after all. By the way, did you see Chicklade reach for a pistol earlier?"

"Aye, I did. I'm not saying he didn't have cause, but what I *am* saying is, I'd give a deal to learn what cause a groom has to go armed. It seems a peaceable enough country." He grinned suddenly. "Not like some I could name."

For once the major failed to respond to the reminder. "So would I give a good deal," he said, as if to himself. "A very good deal."

* * *

Later that same day, Miss Dunraven encountered her groom enjoying another pipe in solitude. She eyed his bland countenance for a moment, then said defensively, as if meeting some unvoiced criticism, "Don't bother to say anything, Joe! But I won't stand by and watch a horse abused."

"I didn't say nothing," Chicklade objected innocently.

She laughed without humor. "You don't have to. At any rate, you've little room to talk. What were you meaning to do, pull a pistol right there in front of everybody? How the devil did you expect to explain that?"

He shrugged. "Thankfully, it wasn't necessary."

She was restless for some reason, which was unlike her. "I still don't like it. Grandfather thinks he's a fool, but I disagree. It seems to me he sees far too much with those sleepy gray eyes of his."

"And here I was thinkin' he's eyes for only one thing," drawled the groom with a certain amusement. As she flushed, he added more practically, "But I'll admit he's likely to prove dangerous. Warned me he plans to be back tomorrow, by the way. I'm to tell Himself."

"Oh, it's intolerable!" she burst out. "Damn Sir James and his tricks! I'll simply have to find some other way to drive him away." She laughed again. "It shouldn't be hard. We can scarcely be what he's used to. At any rate, Sir James is right. He's unlikely to kick his heels willingly here for long."

"I don't know," the groom said thoughtfully. "If you ask me, his lordship didn't strike me as a man easily discouraged."

She looked quickly up at him, then away again. "Oh, the divil fly awa' with him! Which reminds me, I noticed Patch was here this morning, ready to report back to Sir James. Heaven knows how he manages always to be where he's least wanted, for he's never to be found when there's any work to be done. You haven't managed to sniff out any hint of what they're up to yet, have you?''

"Not yet. Where's Master Jamie, by the way? I thought he'd be eager to meet his lordship, at least.''

She flushed again for some reason and said shortly, ''I sent him into town. The last thing we need is for him to develop a hero worship for our unwanted visitor, which he's more than likely to do. Oh, hell and the devil confound it. The only thing we can do is have Jem keep an eye on him at all times while he's here. In the meantime, settle the bay in—but not too comfortably. I don't intend for him to be here long. As for those fool grooms, they should have been horsewhipped, and your precious Lord Simon Grey with them!''

6

The major rose next morning with the dawn, Miss Dunraven and the suspicious goings-on at Dunraven Downs still very much on his mind.

He was determined to regain his ability in the saddle, and had deliberately chosen such an unseasonable hour for his first attempt, since had no desire for any witnesses to his probable humiliation.

A disapproving Aikins had the docile mount they had hired saddled and waiting for him. His own horse was also ready, and the major could tell from the groom's expression that not even a direct order would keep him behind.

By dint of much difficulty and cursing, the major at last managed to haul himself into the saddle, but he was unprepared for the effort it cost him. His still-limited strength was nearly spent by even so minor an effort, and his injured leg had already begun to throb.

He sat breathlessly in the saddle, feeling the sweat strike cool against the dawn air and wondering how he could feel as if he had fought an entire battle, not merely mounted the back of a horse. He was angrily aware of the temptation to give up and finally accept the word of the doctors that he would never ride again. Then furiously he stiffened his spine and, white-lipped with determination, wheeled out of the inn yard and headed out of town, the disapproving Aikins at his heels.

The cool morning air and the slight mist both felt good against his overheated brow, and he tried to ignore the trembling weakness of his thigh. He felt slightly giddy, as if he had been drinking, and made his mind concentrate on the mystery at Dunraven Downs in an effort to steady it.

He couldn't say why he felt so instinctively that something was very wrong there. The whole place and its inhabitants were unconventional, of course, with its slovenly servants and general air of neglect, not to mention the odd behavior of Sir James and his granddaughter. Certainly during neither of his two visits had he been made to feel in the least welcome.

But it went far beyond that. As for that remarkable display yesterday, he had yet to come to terms with it. He had feared he'd have nightmares last night about seeing Cat struck down by slashing hooves. Nor did he begin to understand why the head groom at the Downs evidently went armed.

All in all, it was a most annoying puzzle, and the major had a constitutional dislike of puzzles. It did not take much intellect to divine that Miss Cathleen Dunraven's remarkable rudeness seemed designed for the express purpose of driving him away. But he was damned if he could see what possible threat he could be to her.

It could be, of course, that he was making mountains out of molehills, and she was simply worried about the extra work. But for the price that old blackguard, her grandfather, had extorted from him, she could easily hire half a dozen extra grooms.

Nor did that explain why there was a distinct shadow in those remarkably beautiful blue eyes of hers, or that hard air of defiance about her, as if she had taken too many hard knocks in her short life and meant to see she received no more.

At the thought, the major's hands tightened unconsciously, and he had to soothe his placid mount.

He had repaired to the taproom after dinner last night for the express purpose of culling what gossip he could about the Dunravens. But he had merely attracted curious interest, and received few answers for his pains. The general consensus seemed to be that Sir James Dunraven was on the verge of ruin, and had been for years; but that much had been obvious from the major's first sight of the Downs. Which only made it all the more puzzling why Cat should be trying to drive him away when they so obviously needed the money.

Cat herself had been mentioned only in passing, and with a grudging respect, but whether that was in deference to the fact that Simon was an outsider, he had no way of knowing. He could only ruefully hope that he had not somehow inadvertently betrayed himself by a proprietary interest he had not meant to reveal.

Though he feared it would be no more than the truth if he had. For he was ruefully aware that he was in considerable danger of falling head over heels in love with a difficult and wholly ineligible beauty, based on nothing but a sullen temper and an undoubted witchcraft in the saddle.

Put like that, it sounded ludicrous. But he should have known it had been almost inevitable. He had been rejecting conventional and well-brought-up young ladies for years now, to the despair of his mother and friends. It had begun to seem that he would have an impossible termagant to wive, or no one.

The thought made him laugh out loud, and the clear, untrammeled sound clearly startled both Aikins and his mount. It had been so long since he'd really laughed at anything, but he felt suddenly alive, and absurdly light-hearted. All the dark and gloomy visions of the future that had been haunting him seemed to have lost all power over him, as if they had been nothing but the last vestiges of his lingering fever.

Not even the acute ache in his thigh or the plodding pace of the hired hack beneath him could destroy his newfound sense of well-being. He wanted to race across the heath, as that distant figure was doing, or ride immediately to Dun-raven Downs for the purpose of laying his heart and fortune at Miss Cathleen Dunraven's elegant, indifferent feet.

He laughed again at her probable astonishment. She would think him mad, with good reason, and perhaps it *was* mad to feel this sudden lightheartedness and the conviction that he had at last found a future he had only been searching for all these years.

He was on the verge of obeying Aikins' unspoken desire and turn back, but merely for the prosaic purpose of resting his thigh and eating his breakfast, when something about the figure he had vaguely noticed streaking across the heath on the back of a beautiful black caught his attention and held it.

There were no other riders out at that early hour, and the other had obviously taken advantage of the fact to race his mount at a reckless speed that ignored such mundane considerations as the uneven ground and ever-present rabbit holes. They made a graceful picture, though, and the major had automatically assumed the rider was male, since he was clearly riding astride.

But now something about that proud carriage and the unnatural unity between horse and rider suddenly told him instinctively that the figure was not male at all. Or perhaps she was indeed a witch, and the mere fact that he was thinking about her had conjured her up somehow.

Whichever, a grin lifted the corner of his mouth, and he

pulled to a halt, waiting with a confidence he could not explain for Miss Cathleen Dunraven to overtake him.

Dawn had always been Cat's favorite time of day. The mist crept breast-high across the heath, and the air was pure and cold and suffused with a golden light that always, for a short time at least, made the world look new and possible again.

Folly seemed to share her love for the early-morning hours. It was almost as if they ceased to be separate entities for that short hour before the sun came up and the real world intruded once again. As she clung, crouched over his neck and making no attempt either to guide or to check him, she could feel every breath the black drew into his powerful lungs. She recognized the instinctive hesitation he gave long before she registered any obstacle ahead, and knew the exact moment he bunched his great muscles beneath him to carry them effortlessly over fence or hedge, stream or gully.

They both were fully aware that he could have rid himself of her at any time, as easily as a dog did a troublesome flea. But after his first instinctive lashing out every morning, he seemed to tolerate her slight weight for the sake of his freedom. She sometimes thought it was a temporary truce in the ongoing battle between them for dominance.

At best they shared a queer love-hate relationship that was tempered on both sides by a healthy respect. Folly despised all humans, and had already killed a trainer. In the auction ring where she had first seen him, it had taken five men with whips and goads to hold him down.

Cat had reason to know how useless and dangerous a savage horse was, especially in racing. A killer was a killer, and you would break his heart and your own before you broke his spirit. The only thing to do when you encountered one was to put him down.

She knew that intellectually. But for some reason her heart

had gone out to the magnificent black fighting against such impossible odds, and she had not been able to stand by and watch him humbled by those sadistic brutes. She had bought him for a ridiculously low sum, telling herself he would be good at stud, for the days had long passed when they were able to afford the cream of the yearlings, as they had once done.

Sir James, predictably, had been scathing in his reaction. He had no time for anyone's sentimentality but his own, and a racehorse that couldn't race was less than useless to them. He washed his hands of the whole affair and bluntly recommended the animal be put down at once, instead of throwing good money after bad.

But he also unwittingly had given the black its name. He had called it Cat's Folly in an effort to goad her, but she had found it oddly fitting. She had altered it only to Dunraven's Folly, in a gibe at her grandfather's habit of vaunting his name over everything he touched.

And in the end, of course, she had not been able to resist the challenge of trying to win Folly's trust. She had no desire to do more than that, for she had a sneaking sympathy for the black's mistrust of her fellowmen, and had no intention of trying to break his spirit.

And to a certain extent she had succeeded. Folly would carry her now, but she suspected it was on his terms, not her own. Certainly she was never tempted to relax her vigilance for a moment, or lose sight of the fact that at any moment he could turn killer again.

She suspected the knowledge merely added spice to the struggle for both of them. Whatever the reason, their early-morning rides had come to be the only time in the day when she felt really alive.

Today she had made no attempt to check Folly's bad temper, somehow needing the struggle between them as an outlet for her own dark mood. As a consequence she had allowed him to go farther afield than usual, and the sun was almost completely up before she at last managed to pull him back into a canter, and then, gradually, to a walk.

She reached forward then to stroke his neck, receiving only an attempted nip for her pains. She laughed, noting the way the glossy black sides heaved and the great nostrils flared, gulping in the cold fresh air. She knew he would have gone on tirelessly forever if she had let him. She sometimes wondered if, on his own, he would run until his heart burst.

Her own black hair was tangled hopelessly by now, and her thighs and arms were aching with weariness. But she felt oddly at peace, as if the strange demon within her, whatever it had been, had been vanquished for the moment.

She was on the point of reluctantly turning back, since there were a million things waiting for her to do at home, when her gloved hands froze on the reins. She could see two distant figures on horseback, and like Lord Simon, for some reason she had no trouble at all in knowing instinctively who they were.

Abruptly all her hard-won peace left her, and she spurred forward without thought, too angry at being spied on to weigh the wisdom of her actions.

Both horsemen lifted their heads, but sat without moving as she bore furiously down upon them.

She pulled up only at the last minute, her hair blowing wildly and her breast heaving. "*How dare you spy on me*?" she cried.

The groom looked rather startled at the accusation, but Lord Simon merely smiled at her in an annoyingly happy way, as if he were delighted to see her. "I'm sorry. I wasn't aware this was private property."

For some reason his logic only added to her anger. "You know perfectly well it isn't! But why else would you be up at such an absurd hour? I thought men of your type slept until noon.''

His face darkened a little at the unmistakable insult in her tone, but he merely said calmly, ''No doubt you're right, Miss Dunraven. Unfortunately, this is the first time I've been on horseback since my accident. I preferred to make my first humiliating attempts without half the town watching me make a fool of myself.''

She at least had the grace to feel ashamed of herself, but said curtly, ''Even so, I would recommend you remain closer to home. The heath can be dangerous, and even with your groom to accompany you, if you took a fall you could lie hurt for a long time before anyone could reach you.''

''I'll keep that in mind. As a matter of fact, I'm glad you brought the subject up, for I was just thinking exactly the same thing. You're easily the best rider I've ever seen, but that black looks anything but reliable. Were you to take a toss some morning, it might be hours before you were found, as you so rightly pointed out.''

He only voiced what Jamie and Chicklade had been saying for months, and in even stronger terms. But for some reason the major's mild criticism annoyed her out of all proportion to the offense. Especially since Folly chose that moment to protest the delay and the stranger's presence by jibbing and making a spirited attempt to unseat her.

She was never in any danger, especially as tired as Folly was by then. But the major, conditioned no doubt by years of inbred chivalry and having to protect indifferent feminine equestriennes under his escort, reacted instinctively. He grabbed the bit below her hands and pulled Folly's head around sharply.

He was, had he known it, only adding to her danger, for Folly never tolerated another's hand on his bit. But Cat brought him under control with one iron hand, her eyes flashing fire, and deliberately lashed out without thought at that offending hand.

"Damn you! How *dare* you!" she cried imperiously. "The day I can't handle my own horse is the day I give up riding completely."

She had reacted instinctively, even as he had done. But she was surprised by the speed of his response. Until now she had seen only the cripple and the civilian, and so had forgotten that he was undoubtedly honed by years of danger into split-second action. Before she had time to grasp his intent, he had grabbed the thong of her whip and twisted it out of her hands, causing Folly to rear again in anger and fright.

His own placid mount, startled into unprecedented nervousness, also shied. Though Cat was certainly never in any real danger, the major, with his stiff leg and awkward posture, was not so fortunate. Cat saw him wince, as if in sudden pain, and swear under his breath. For a moment it looked dangerously as if he must be thrown to land directly under the feet of one or both of the horses.

7

Then, with an almost superhuman effort, the major managed to retain his seat, though at what cost, Cat didn't like to think. His face was pale under his tan as he at last brought his mount under control and said breathlessly, "Sorry—! That was indeed presumptuous of me. Especially under the circumstances. It appears I can scarcely control my own mount, let alone yours."

Cat was badly shaken, for she had not intended to go so far. Nor could she suppress an unwilling admiration for him in that moment. She wanted to reach out to him—or apologize: both of which were equally foolish. Unwittingly or not, he was her enemy, and it was dangerous to forget it.

So she made herself say coolly, "Are you all right?"

Abruptly he laughed out loud, and she noticed resentfully that he had a very nice laugh. His eyes crinkled attractively at the corners, and his somewhat careworn look was momentarily banished, so that he looked more as he must have done as a handsome and assured young officer. "If you mean am I hurt, nothing but my pride, I fear, Miss Dunraven. And I'm beginning to think you are good for me. It seems I was getting impossibly set up in my own conceit without even knowing it. But at the risk of completing my discomfiture, may I ask why you dislike me so much? I'm usually considered the mildest of fellows, you know."

He was watching her with an odd, alert air that she found strangely disturbing, as if the answer really mattered to him. It made her self-conscious, and suddenly absurdly aware of her windblown appearance and boy's clothing. She had always despised feminine vanity and cared little how she looked. She conformed to certain conventions simply to avoid adding any further fuel to her reputation; but for these early-morning rides, when she seldom encountered anyone, she had long since abandoned her skirts as dangerous encumbrances.

But Major Lord Simon Grey, in an immaculate blue coat and buff breeches and shining top boots, and with his handsome, well-bred air, reminded her furiously that she must look like nothing so much as the vulgar Irish harridan he must already think her.

The awareness added to her discomfort, and she responded icily, "You flatter yourself, my lord. I don't dislike you any more than I do any other absentee owner who thinks to dabble briefly in racing for his own amusement and will soon grow bored with it."

"Ah, yes. My 'type,' as you called it," he said easily. "I can see your mind is obviously made up, so it will do little good to assure you that I have no such intention. In fact, my friends would tell you that I have rather the reputation of refusing to give up on anything I've undertaken, even to the point of obstinacy."

The impression that the conversation was somehow deeper than she thought persisted, as if they were speaking on two different levels; but she made herself dismiss it. "But then, it's all nothing but a game to men like you, isn't it?" she demanded contemptuously.

He looked annoyingly amused. "Forgive me. I thought

that's what it was; a sport. I'm afraid after the life I've lived the last ten years, I can't take it as seriously as you obviously do.''

She flushed. "Very well! If you really want to know why I dislike you, then I'll tell you. I despise anyone like you and your father who have too much money and too little sense, and think to take up the sport on a lark, because you're bored. If you win a few races, you'll think it's all very easy, and pocket the rewards and congratulations without giving a thought to those who did the real work and endured the heartbreak for you.

"And if you lose, you'll shrug and pass easily on to the next whim that takes your fancy. And in either case you won't give a damn about the sport itself. You'll close your eyes to the unpleasant sides of it, telling yourself such things have always been there. You and people like you never—"

Abruptly she broke off, realizing by the faint puzzled frown in his eyes that she had come close to saying too much and betraying herself in the bargain.

"That may be," he said easily at last. "I won't bother to try to dispute your accusations, for it seems your mind is already made up. You're obviously as quick with your tongue as you are with your whip, Miss Dunraven. But has it never occurred to you that not everyone can be neatly labeled and despised on the strength of your particular prejudices? My father may be all of those things. I don't know. But I'm not my father, any more than you are your grandfather. Do you care to be tarred with his brush?''

"I am tarred with it! Do you think when I ride into town people's eyes don't follow me, wondering if I'll speak with an Irish brogue? But why am I wasting my time trying to explain to you? I can only repeat that I despise you and men like you, and everything you stand for!"

His eyes were steady on her, and there was a telltale flush

on his cheeks, but he said ruefully, "In that case, something tells me that is not the right moment to propose to you, Miss Dunraven. I can only beg your forgiveness and leave you to the privacy I've so rudely interrupted."

Her eyes widened and she gasped; then her face suffused with color. She had insulted him and he had retaliated in kind, choosing the surest way to return the favor, knowing what her reputation was. She was tempted to slash out at him again, but satisfied herself by spurring Folly with a furious heel and leaving the major where he sat.

Though she did not turn around, she was conscious of his eyes following her as if they burned a hole in her back.

Simon was left to make his way back to town more slowly, his groom for once maintaining a discreet silence at his side.

The major was ignominiously aware that he had made a fool of himself. He certainly had had no intention of blurting out that foolish proposal. If the sight of Cat in boy's clothing, streaking across the heath on the back of a beautiful, dangerous black, had somehow settled what few doubts he had remaining, he was ruefully aware that his chosen did not seem to have suffered a similar revelation. So far she had yet to betray even common politeness in his company, and gave every indication of disliking him heartily.

He did not think himself so set up in his own conceit that it had never occurred to him that the woman he finally fell head over heels in love with would not return his regard. But he could not help thinking that Miss Cathleen Dunraven's dislike seemed to him to be out of all proportion to the situation.

In fact, it was beginning to be borne in upon him that there was something seriously wrong there. He had a sharply honed sense of danger, developed over ten years of campaigning, and he was beginning to fear that something more lay behind the seeming chip on his tiresome love's shoulder than mere contempt for his class. He was not ordinarily a fanciful man, but he could not quite dismiss the unpleasant notion that behind Cat's belligerence there lurked unmistakable fear. And he could only wonder what it was that so fearless and daunting a young lady was afraid of.

As for her habit of streaking across the heath dressed in boy's clothes and astride a black he wouldn't have cared to ride himself, even before his injury, he was beginning to think it was more than time that she was broken to bridle, as her grandfather so colorfully put it, before she succeeded in breaking her beautiful, defiant neck.

The major was to find out for himself at least one of the things Cat was afraid of sooner than he had anticipated, for when he drove out to the Downs later that afternoon, he found her in one of the empty box stalls fighting off the determined advances of a flashily attractive man.

Her attacker was well-dressed, but something in his bearing and face bespoke the self-made man. He also seemed to have imbibed rather too freely at luncheon, for even as the major watched, he backed Cat into a corner. "Don't play the innocent with me, you little termagant!" he said thickly. "I'll have your answer now, or the deal's off."

Cat seemed to be more angry than afraid of him. "You're drunk!" she said contemptuously. "You'll have my answer when I'm ready to give it, and not before."

The other growled something unpleasant under his breath. "You'll not keep me dangling on a string like you do the rest of those fools, you little tease! I know both your grandfather's games and yours, and I'll have something on account now."

Abruptly he lunged, managing to capture Cat's hands and

wedge them behind her back before clumsily trying to kiss her.

Simon waited for no more, but hauled him back by his coat, saying harshly, "The lady doesn't seem to appreciate your advances."

He succeeded in pulling the man off, owing more to the element of surprise and the close quarters of the stall than anything else. But the man turned rapidly on Simon, mingled surprise and fury in his face. "What the . . . ? Who the devil are *you*?"

"Major Simon Grey, very much at Miss Dunraven's service," said the major mockingly. "And if you'll accept a word of advice, I'd suggest you try less brutal tactics next time. You might find them more effective."

The man reddened angrily, but then, as he took in Simon's stick and obviously weak leg, he began to laugh. "And are you going to make me if I don't choose to take your advice?" he demanded.

Simon's face betrayed nothing but amused contempt, but his senses were alert and his mind racing. The man was considerably heavier than he was, and in his present condition the major knew that in any kind of fight he was likely to come off a very poor second.

Still, it never even occurred to him to back down. "If I have to," he said pleasantly. "It seems time someone taught you some manners."

Cat had fallen back, panting a little, but predictably she did not scream or withdraw in horror as most women would have done. "Both of you get out!" she cried angrily. "As for you," she added, rounding on the major, "I don't need you or anyone else to fight my battles for me."

He spared a moment to smile down into her furious eyes. "I'm beginning to think it's time someone did," he said.

"Now, get out of here, there's a good girl. You are definitely in the way."

She flushed, but stood her ground. "No, *you* get out! Both of you! I won't be fought over like some town trollop."

Both men ignored her as if she hadn't spoken. "Ah, I'm beginning to see," said the beefy man unpleasantly. "Only I'd be careful if I was you, Cat. I somehow doubt he's willing to pay quite as high a price as I am, my dear. Such sprigs of fashion are seldom interested in marriage, you know, and the last time I heard, that was the price for your . . . er . . . favors."

Simon laughed, completely untouched by the insult. " 'Miss Dunraven' to you. And if that's what you think me, I should be flattered. But *Miss Dunraven*"—he subtly underlined the name—"already knows what my intentions are, for I proposed to her this morning."

As the other's jaw dropped, Cat said furiously, "Both of you are disgusting! As for you, it would serve you right if I left you to be beaten up by Baggett!"

"Ah, I was wondering who he was," said Simon cheerfully. "As for being beaten up by him, it's possible, but I wouldn't put any money on it if I were you."

Baggett was looking between them plainly at something of a loss. But at last he said belligerently, "Myself, I never pass up a sure thing. As for *Miss Dunraven*, I had no idea she was so clever. Or do you think to turn her up sweet until you're finished with her and can disappear? You somehow don't look like the type who would stoop to wedding the penniless granddaughter of a vulgar Irish bogman—even for sport."

Simon waited for no more. He had been a fairly decent boxer at one time and could only rely on the element of surprise once more. Before the other could divine his intention, he dropped him with a surprisingly neat right hook to th ejaw and followed with a blow across the back of the head with his stick that would—he devoutly hoped—knock him briefly unconscious.

But even the brief effort left him breathing harder than he would have liked. He ignored it in the surge of momentary triumph and the familiar excitement of battle that had him in its grip. "I would suggest you get out of here—now, Miss Dunraven!" he said breathlessly. "I managed to take your friend by surprise, but you are very much in the way. It would be better for both of us if you weren't here when he comes to."

She was oddly pale now, and her own breast was rising and falling for some reason. "Are you *mad*?" she whispered. "Do you know who he is?"

"No. Should I?"

She almost threw up her hands. "You . . . I can't . . . I'm beginning to think I'm the one who's mad! He's a notorious bully! And even if he weren't, what possible chance do you think you'd have against him in your condition?"

Simon grinned at her, still on top of the world. "Perhaps very little, which is why I'd prefer you not to be here," he confessed. "For just once in your life, Miss Dunraven, do as you're told! And hurry. He's already stirring. He must have a harder head than I'd thought."

Still she stood there. "Oh, the devil! I should take you at your word and leave you with him!" she raged. "But I refuse to have your death upon my conscience. I . . . Please, just go! I'm in no danger, I tell you. I can handle him."

"It looked it." It seemed to Simon that she was not as indifferent to him as she would have him believe, and at the moment he felt as if he could have dealt with a dozen bullies, weak leg or no weak leg. In fact, if it weren't for Cat's presence and the lowering suspicion that he'd soon be laughing out of the other side of his mouth, he would almost have relished the coming fight. He'd been inactive for far too long and had needed just such a turn-up.

Baggett had sat up by now, shaking his head, but still seemed slightly befuddled. "What the . . . was it *you* who hit me, damn you?" he demanded disbelievingly.

"It was," Simon said readily. "I would suggest you apologize to Miss Dunraven and leave quietly now. And don't come back until you've sobered up."

Baggett growled and lunged to his feet. There was a dangerous light in his eyes, but he was handicapped by his anger and his contempt for his opponent, and Simon easily parried his wild swing. He used the wall of the stall to brace himself and held his cane as a weapon, but he was ruefully aware, even as he managed to land a satisfying blow to the man's too-handsome face, that he would soon be spent.

This time Baggett did not go down, though his nose started to bleed. The major's knuckles were bruised and his balance extremely precarious, but he waited, not pressing the fight, but poised to counter any move his opponent might make.

"Stop it! Stop it, damn you!" cried Cat, forced against a wall of the stall by the fight. But then she somewhat diluted her appeal by adding waspishly, "I hope you both kill each other!"

She might as well have spared her breath, for neither combatant had time to pay her the slightest attention. Baggett reeled, and wiped the blood out of his mouth. Then he swung wildly again, this time the red light of murder in his eyes.

Again Simon was able to avoid the full force of the blow, though he could feel his weak leg starting to tremble from the strain of his weight. It was obvious to him by now that his opponent possessed little science. Six months ago it would have been easy to use the fool's own weight and his fury to defeat him.

Unfortunately, it was not six months ago, and the major knew he could not hope to last much longer. He managed to feint and block the next blow aimed at his own face, and delivered another, solid punch. But this time there was almost no strength behind it, and he was not surprised to receive a blow in return that split his own lip.

He was just wondering fatalistically how much of a fool he'd make of himself when both men were brought rudely back to reality by a shock of cold water thrown directly in their faces.

8

"I said stop it, both of you!" Cat stood fearlessly before them, another pail already lifted in readiness. "The first one who makes a move gets another dose."

Simon had gasped and fallen backward, almost oversetting as his weak leg buckled beneath him; and Baggett, who had received the lion's share of the water, was momentarily blinded.

The latter swore and tried to clear his streaming eyes, his clothes soaked and his temper not improved by the dash of cold water.

The major reluctantly began to laugh. They both looked ridiculous with the water dripping off them and Cat standing over them like an avenging fury. "I should have known. Is there anything that fazes you, Miss Dunraven?"

Baggett looked far less amused. The water mixed with blood from his battered face to stain his clothes, but it at least seemed to have sobered him slightly. "You should be grateful you have her skirts to hide behind, Grey," he snarled. "But there's one thing you seem to have missed, Miss Dunraven is going to marry me."

Simon's heart leapt, but he made himself glance calmly at Cat. "Is that true?"

She hesitated, and her lashes swept down to hide the vibrant blue of her eyes. Simon's breathing seemed to be suspended as he waited for her answer.

Then at last she took a deep breath and lifted her head. "No," she said defiantly. "It isn't! I haven't given him my answer yet."

Baggett swore and looked slowly from one to the other. "I'm beginning to see the lay of the land," he sneered at last. "It seems you've even more ambition than I thought. Does the title make up for him being only half a man? But I warn you, don't think to come crying to me when he's thrown you over. I take no man's leavings."

Simon had once again forgotten his handicap in the desire to ram the filthy words back down Baggett's oily throat. He started forward again, but Cat literally threw herself at him, holding him back. "Get out of here!" she panted. "And don't ever dare to threaten me again!"

Baggett hesitated, then shrugged and stalked off.

Cat continued to hold Simon back with the full force of her weight, as if even now she feared he would go after him. "Are you completely mad?" she stormed. "I'm beginning to think I should have let him knock some sense into you."

Simon laughed, feeling slightly light-headed. "Why didn't you? It would have been one way of getting rid of me, and that is what you want, isn't it?"

"Yes! Oh, God! You are . . . are you hurt?" she asked reluctantly.

"Only my pride, sweetheart. This, on top of my adventures on horseback this morning, seems to have made for a full day. You're not really considering marrying that bully, are you?"

"Do you always blunder in and ruin other people's lives?" she demanded bitterly. "Give me your handkerchief."

He smiled and handed it to her. She took it and dabbed

at the cut on his mouth with scant gentleness. She looked both beautiful and extremely furious, and he wanted to take her in his arms and kiss away the ill temper in her eyes.

"I knew you would be nothing but trouble!" she continued to scold. "Why can't you go away? Your family shouldn't even let you out by yourself, for you obviously need a keeper!"

He endured her ministrations for a moment, then stopped her hand with his own. "Perhaps. But not until you tell me what that villain is holding over you."

"This is all still just a joke to you, isn't it?" she demanded. "A lark to pass a few boring weeks! Only you may find it turning into less of a jest, for Daniel Baggett is an extremely dangerous man. Not even your name and wealth can protect you from everything."

He turned up her face and stared into her blazing eyes. "I guess I can't expect you to take me seriously yet. In fact, I'm almost as bowled over by what's happened between us as you are. But I can assure you this is no jest. I'm in deadly earnest for perhaps the first time in my life."

She stiffened, and then pulled away with little care for his weak leg, and left him without another word.

But once safely outside, and away from prying eyes, she collapsed weakly against a stable wall, her eyes closed. "Oh, damn you!" she whispered at last. *"Damn you!"*

As the major more slowly made his way back to his curricle, limping more heavily than ususal, the elder Chicklade's voice stopped him. "Are you all right, my lord?"

The major turned to regard him. For once the groom met his eyes steadily, with none of his usual bland evasion. "That depends," he answered at last. "Who is Baggett and what's he holding over your mistress?"

The groom stiffened and dropped his eyes. "Daniel Baggett owns the next estate," he said at last, reluctantly. "But if you want to know anything more than that, I'm thinkin' you'd best ask Miss Cat."

"I have asked her. She told me she can handle her own affairs. But from what I've seen so far, you'll give me leave to doubt it. I've met her grandfather and don't expect much there, but what of her brother? Doesn't he care what becomes of her?"

"Master Jamie is devoted to his sister. But I warned you Miss Cat was a law unto herself."

Simon laughed without humor. "So I'm beginning to see. Is it usual for a groom to go armed in these parts, by the way?"

When he received no answer, the major added deliberately, "Well, I mean to take a hand now. And while we're on the subject, I don't care for Miss Cat's habit of riding out alone on the back of that dangerous-looking black of hers. From now on I'd suggest you or your son find an excuse to accompany her. Is that clear?"

Chicklade's expression remained discreetly bland, but there was a hint of satisfaction in his voice as he answered dryly, "Perfectly clear, Major."

When Cat wearily entered the house five minutes later, her grandfather was waiting for her. "I hear that spalpeen Baggett has dared to show his face here again!" he said angrily.

She wanted only to reach the seclusion of her room, but she made herself stiffen her spine and turn to face her grandfather. "I'm surprised the news took so long to reach you," she retorted sarcastically. "Your spies must be slipping."

"But then, it's little enough I'd know of me own doings

if I relied upon you and Jamie for news," he grumbled. "Patch is my eyes and ears, now that I can't get about much mesel' any longer."

"He's also your tool in any of your more nefarious schemes. Don't try to fool me. Just take care that the town fathers don't oblige me by running him off before I can. Danny is bad enough, without him littering the countryside with his redheaded bastards."

Sir James pretended to be shocked. "Now, Caity, I won't have ye usin' such language. What should you be knowin' of bastards, I'm wonderin', redheaded or otherwise? And don't try to change the subject. What was that divil doin' here, when I've made it plain I won't have 'im on the place?"

She could not tell if he was playing with her or really had not heard the outcome of the confrontation, but for some reason she had no desire for him to know it. "What do you think he was doing here?" she countered. "He came to see what he could nose out about Lord Simon's bay, of course."

Sir James chuckled, as if well-pleased at something. "Well, I hope ye sent 'im off with a flea in his ear for his pains. Which reminds me, Chicklade tells me the colt seems promisin'."

She shrugged and tried to ease her weary shoulders. "Joe is optimistic. He's fast enough, but he's too inclined to take out his temper on his jockey, and he's inconsistent on the track."

"Aye, well, I hope ye'll have him ready for the Two Thousand Guineas," he threw out casually. "I've assured his lordship we will."

Slowly she turned to face him. "I should have known you had something like that up your sleeve," she said with dangerous quiet at last. "But *why*? What the devil do you hope to gain?"

When she received no answer, she added in a harder voice, "And what happens when he discovers the truth about how we've cheated him?"

"Cheated him? Ye've just said the horse stands no chance of winning." He was all innocence.

She had always known there was no besting him. "I'm finally beginning to see. I wondered why Baggett was so interested in Lord Simon's horse. In fact, Joe tells me the bay's attracting considerable attention in town for an untried colt. And don't trouble to assume that innocent air with me. It's been obvious to me from the first that you were up to something. I just couldn't guess what. But I should have known it would be . . . worthy of you!"

"It's a sad day when a man has so disrespectful a grand-daughter," said Sir James, mournfully shaking his head. "By the by, did ye know our friend Baggett is meaning to run two entries?"

Her eyes widened despite herself. "Two?" It never occurred to her to doubt her grandfather's sources.

"Aye, I thought that would interest you. He's keepin' the second under wraps, of course, but Patch got it from one of his lads, though it cost him a bottle of blue ruin to do it. And a most curious horse it would appear to be, for it seems to have materialized out of nowhere and has been moved around a suspicious amount in its short life. It's said to be out of stables up north, but it's been raced abroad as a two-year-old, and since it's been back in this country, has seldom stayed in one place long enough to be recognized. It's almost as if friend Baggett's tryin' to keep anyone from gettin' too good a look at it or following its career too closely. But then, like you, lass, I've a strangely suspicious nature, I fear."

She frowned. "You think it's a ringer?"

"Aye, a four-year-old run as a three-year-old. It's not the first time it's been tried. Not that anyone'll be able to prove it," he answered cheerfully. "Baggett's too clever for that. But he might be findin' he's not so clever as he thinks."

"I see. And you obviously intend to muddy the waters even further by adding another unknown to the tangle—hence Lord Simon's horse. Which one are you meaning to back?" she added cynically.

"Ah, well, that rather depends on which nag carries my friend Baggett's money, doesn't it?" said Sir James innocently. "If he's wise, he won't broadcast the fact, and will take very good care to scatter his bets, but you must admit the addition of a second entry makes the field a good deal more interestin'. Particularly since he had the favorite already."

"You think he actually means to nobble his own favorite? You know Philanderer is his pride and joy. He was boasting to me only this morning that he was sure to win."

"Ah, which makes me think he means to do just that. But then, he'd not be the first man to sacrifice his pride in pursuit of more favorable odds, I'm thinkin'. Philanderer is already the odds-on favorite, so Baggett'll do little better than take the purse if he wins."

Her mind was grappling frantically with all the repercussions of her grandfather's news. "So you mean to beat Baggett at his own game? Well, I've no objection to seeing him taken down a peg or two. But you know what will happen if he thinks Conquerer any sort of threat. He'll stop at nothing to get to him. Or was that part of your plan as well?" she demanded angrily.

"Nay, lass! I won't have you talk like that, for I've niver yet stooped to harmin' horses, nor will I."

She was unimpressed by his protestations of innocence. "Even without that, it's a dirty trick, and you know it. I suppose you had it in mind all along."

He didn't deny it. "Aye, well, it's a dirty business, I'm

thinkin'. No great harm will come of it, and possibly a great deal of good.''

She felt too weary to deal with her grandfather now. She wanted only to be alone to come to terms with the last hour. "No great harm?" She laughed a little wildly. "I doubt Lord Simon would agree with you. But I warn you now, I won't have the bay endangered. If it comes to that, I'll go straight to Lord Simon and tell him everything, whatever the consequences. And then I'll marry Baggett just to spite you! And you know me well enough to know I mean what I say."

"What the divil's got into you of late?" Sir James demanded irritably.

"Nothing. Absolutely nothing. But I meant what I said."

He was watching her closely in a way she mistrusted. "And what of Folly?" he asked softly. "Or are you becomin' so scrupulous ye've decided to give up on your own plans?"

She turned away and closed her eyes briefly. "No, I haven't given up. It seems we're two of a kind, Grandfather, just as you said."

9

Cat climbed the stairs to her room, but she knew she could not escape her thoughts so easily.

She should not have been surprised by her grandfather's revelations, for she had known he was up to something. At any rate, she had always known what he was, and no one knew better than she how dirty a sport racing was. Spies were everywhere, and fortunes made or lost on a groom or trainer talking too freely in his cups, or a piece of information falling into the wrong hands.

Worse, there were few rules and little enforcement of the few there were. Jockeys were bribed or disabled, mounts interfered with or denied clean starts, and even poisoned on occasion, for right there in Newmarket there had been a rash of poisonings of public water troughs in the last few years. Half a dozen horses had been killed, and more than one owner ruined, but they had never managed to find the culprit. Nor was it surprising when such exploits were treated almost as heroic by the worst elements of the turf.

In the face of such determination, not even armed guards posted around the clock before a race could stop anyone really determined to throw it. And the fact that it was supposed to be a gentleman's sport prevented the naive and wealthy absentee owners, like Lord Simon Grey and his noble father, from having to acknowledge the darker, far more sinister side to the sport.

She was sick of it. She had worked in the stables from the time she could first ride, at a precociously early age, and had more or less managed them for years now, ever since Sir James's health had begun to fail.

But if she was sick of it, what other life was there open to her? Marriage to Lord Simon Grey? Aye, that was a laugh.

She had known instinctively from the beginning that he was dangerous, but she hadn't then known exactly how insidious the danger would prove to be. She had feared he meant to interfere with her plans; but she hadn't guessed then that for some reason Lord Simon Grey, with his charm and deceptively easy manner, among all the hundreds of men she had met in her life, would be the one with the power to make her forget all her hard-won resolve.

It was absurd. Were things ten times different than they were, life had long ago taught her that dreams were nothing but a weakness, especially for a woman. They only sapped your determination and betrayed you into abandoning reality for a dangerous half-world of chimeras and wishful thinking. Unfortunately, Cat knew that until now she had never experienced for herself the ease with which a warm smile and the laughter in a pair of shrewd gray eyes could undermine one's defenses so disastrously.

Damn him anyway! Cat had always imagined herself safe from such feminine frailties. She knew far too well what a weakness love could be. Her own mother had married beneath her and lived to bitterly regret it. For years she had struggled against the invidious charm of her husband's careless ways. Once she had found the courage to leave him; but he had always had only to smile at her and she was lost, and they had both known it.

Well, in the end he had broken both her heart and her spirit, and she had died in a strange land she hated. Nor had she even had the comfort of knowing that she had had any impact on her tormentor, for like Sir James, Cat's father had been gay and irresponsible and wholly without a heart of his own.

Cat had always sworn she would never fall into such a trap herself. In her world, determination and ruthlessness were all that mattered, and she intended to have both in full measure.

It was therefore doubly dangerous folly to allow herself even for a moment to contrast wedding Lord Simon, with his gentleness and instinctive chivalry, and marrying the bully and braggart Daniel Baggett. Lord Simon Grey, with his wealth and charm and quiet good manners, was as far above her as the sun in the sky.

Baggett was far more in her league, and the chances were high that she would end with no choice but to wed him—if, after today, even that choice were still open to her. As he had so unkindly pointed out that morning, she should be grateful that his offer included marriage. She was not in any position to hold out if he had another, less savory arrangement in mind.

No, Baggett, curse his vile tongue, had spoken no less than the truth earlier. Were Lord Simon madly in love with her, she was scarcely fit to be introduced to their graces the Duke and Duchess of Salford as a future daughter-in-law, and they all three knew it.

Aye, she could see it now as if it were etched on the wall of her bedchamber, were he to produce her as a potential bride. The shock and the politely veiled disapproval in their graces' faces; the raised brows and carefully measured words. Then the delicate questions about her background and the humiliating necessity of choosing between honesty and self-betrayal.

They would be far too wise to raise any objections in her presence, of course, so she would be spared that, at least. She had seen the Duke of Salford and Lord Simon's brother Denbigh on numerous occasions, and knew both to be well-bred men of reason, ungiven to emotional outbursts or injudicious actions.

No doubt they would even be measured in their response to Lord Simon, fearing to alienate him. But their words would be all the more damning for their very lack of passion.

And they had only to speak the truth, God knew, without any need for embroidery. She had been the intimate of touts and grooms and jockeys all her life, and had the further disadvantage of being the granddaughter of a man who had so deliberately obscured his origins that not even she was certain which of the various stories he liked to tell was the true one.

She might have gained a reluctant acceptance among jockeys, trainers, and some of the wealthy owners because of her undoubted skill with horses and her sharp tongue. But that did not extend to their wives and daughters. A few idle young bucks now and then were misled by her grandfather's reputation and her own free behavior into regarding her as fair game. But her unladylike temper and Jamie's jealous protection usually sent them off in search of easier conquests. But she had had to endure more than one such humiliating scene as Lord Simon had interrupted, and had had to learn to take care of herself.

And she had long ago accepted that if by some miracle she were to come into a fortune tomorrow, she was scarcely fit, at this late date, for any other life. The genteel gossip and stitchery of more respectable women was not for her, for she would find it as exhausting and confining as they would find the life she led distasteful and shocking.

No, it was absurd and dangerous to dream such dreams, even for a moment. Then she laughed bitterly. Especially in light of how they were cheating Lord Simon. Aye, that would make pretty hearing, wouldn't it? *I love you but I've been stealing you blind. I am as slippery as my grandfather, for I learned desperation and cheating and lying from the day I was born, but I never meant to hurt you.*

And what choice had she, after all? She knew he was attracted to her. She had seen it too many times in men's eyes to mistake the warmth of that look. But nothing would come of it, despite that mad proposal. Whether or not he had done it to insult her or merely to pay her back a little for her own rudeness, they both knew he would be a fool to think of marriage.

He might, of course, merely be in line for a little light flirtation to take him out of his present boredom. He might even hope for something more, given her reputation. But he would not throw himself away on her. And she had long since ceased believing in knights in shining armor and the fairy-tale promise of happily ever after. In her world men were far more likely to be brutal, both in passion and in life.

But before today she could at least reassure herself that she was drawn only to Lord Simon's charm and that well-bred assurance that seemed peculiarly his own, and that she would quickly get over him once he was gone again. He had the knack of making those he talked to feel that they had his entire attention, and that could be dangerously flattering, especially to one of her limited experience and background. He seemed to invite others to join in the laughter always lurking at the back of his eyes, and he looked at her as if she were a puzzle that he badly wanted to decipher.

Aye, in her defense, she had had little hope of holding out against the invidious lure of such a man. But she had known only the charming exterior, the polished face he showed the world, after all. Such an attraction had more fascination than anything else about it, and thus could be more easily dismissed.

But that was before she had seen him exhibit such cheerful courage this afternoon as she had doubted existed outside the realm of fairy tales or the marbled covers of romantic novels. Without hesitation he had stood up to the larger Baggett, in spite of his weak leg, and seemed to think it only what anyone else would have done under the circumstances.

He might even believe it, but she knew far better. He had smiled at her in that dangerously warm way of his and said it was past time someone helped her. But in her world, to trust anyone was dangerous, and more likely to be repaid with betrayal than anything else.

She had been furious, with both Lord Simon and herself, and petrified with fear for him. He did not know Baggett the way she did. The man was a bully, unlikely to allow either Lord Simon's handicap or his position to deter his desire for revenge at being made to look foolish before her.

Baggett had made his fortune running gaming hells in London, and was an intimate of all the worst sharps and thieves and touts. He was ten times worse than her grandfather had ever been, but just enough of a reminder of Sir James's own past to make her grandfather hate him with a single-minded passion that was unlike him.

Baggett, for his part, was merely amused by this enmity, and was biding his time before he took all before him—the Downs and everything else, including her. He held a note on the Downs that he had not hesitated to use to try to force her into marriage, and unless a miracle occurred, he would succeed. She might have grown weary of the life and longed to escape, but she loved her grandfather too well to see him completely ruined.

Unfortunately, she had blundered badly this morning in

letting Baggett guess that her long-frozen heart had been thawed at last. He would make her pay for that, and she did not like to think what ingenious methods he would find to do so. Nor, she suspected, would he now rest until he had defeated Lord Simon as well. And her grandfather had played straight into his hands with his latest schemes.

Which brought her back to the only subject that really mattered. She should have known Sir James would find some way to put Lord Simon to good use. She *had* known, in fact, but she lacked her grandfather's devious brain, and so had not hit on the one thing that was needed to turn the whole already impossible situation into something far worse.

She could warn Lord Simon, of course, and put an end to the game before it was too late. But Sir James knew her too well, it seemed. Were she to do so, all her grandfather's schemes would be defeated, certainly. But so would her own slender hopes. And hope was the only thing she had left to cling to.

As for Baggett's ringer, it merely made the game more dangerous. It was not unknown for someone to bring in a ringer—a horse whose origins had been clouded enough to disguise its age or to misrepresent it as another, younger horse. There were as many ways to throw a race as there were devious minds to devise them—from pulling a horse, to interfering with it beforehand, to denying it a clean run. But one of the cleverest was to run a four-year-old in a race for three-year-olds. The older horse was stronger and faster and inevitably had an enormous advantage. The trouble, of course, was in keeping the horse's true identity a secret.

But there, too, the laxity of turf practice made it far easier than it should have been. There might be suspicions, as now, but the Jockey Club seldom consented to involve itself until or unless the disputed horse won. And even then it was up to the second- and third-place finishers to lodge a formal complaint. If an owner were clever, as Baggett was, the charges could be impossible to prove.

That should have made her feel better, for in truth, as Sir James had pointed out, Lord Simon's Conqueror stood little chance of winning. But she knew that was merely a sop thrown to her inconvenient conscience. There was no excuse for what her grandfather intended. And she—God help her— intended far worse.

She laughed again without humor. So much for her dreams. She could either betray Lord Simon's trust or sacrifice all hope of escaping Baggett's net. And in either case she stood no chance of winning at all.

10

In the meantime, quite by accident, the major was making the acquaintance of Cat's brother, Jamie.

On his return to Newmarket, he had found himself oddly restless, and had gone out to walk it off, his thoughts full of Cat. She had softened briefly toward him this afternoon, but it was galling to know she had felt the need to rescue him from her assailant, instead of the other way round.

As for the man named Baggett, every warning instinct in Simon was alert to danger. He did not fear the man himself, but it was obvious that he represented some considerable threat to Cat. And Simon would have given a good deal to know what that was.

Unfortunately, Cat was too proud and stubborn to admit anything, and her groom wasn't talking either, no doubt out of a mislaid sense of loyalty.

It eased Simon's fears considerably to know that Chicklade was there to keep an eye on her, with his steady gaze and the pistol he seemed always to carry with him. Simon was beginning to see why, now. But Chicklade did not have the power, or chose not to use it, to persuade Cat not to expose herself needlessly. Those early-morning rides, for one thing, were even more dangerous in the light of what Simon now knew. But any more mention of them by him would only alienate her still further.

As for her relatives, Simon was fast losing his amused tolerance for Sir James's eccentricities. He was obviously the one to control his granddaughter, but he seemed to make no effort to do so. As for protecting her, Simon was beginning to think neither her grandfather nor her brother knew the meaning of the word. Certainly in the world he was used to, where young women were protected and sheltered from every unpleasantness and kept completely innocent of life's harsher realities, Cat's life seemed incredible to him. According to her groom, she had been exposed to the world of racing as a toddler, and had been running the stables for years. It was little wonder she was wary of trust and cynical of everyone's intentions. Or that she had learned to be stubbornly self-sufficient and determined to rely on no one.

It was not a way of life that appealed to him, and he felt a certain profound pity mixed in with his other deep and growing emotions where Cat was concerned. He would have liked nothing better than to carry her off and keep her safe, away from all threats and harm and disillusion. Unfortunately, the fair maiden not only refused to be rescued, which was hardly a respectable ending to any fairy tale, but also seemed to consider him as much a threat as anyone else. And it was damnable that he could neither help her nor get her to confide in him, and that so far he had only succeeded in adding to her troubles.

He supposed that a cynic might argue that, having found himself suddenly useless and without a goal in life, he had latched on to the notion of playing knight-errant as a sop to his own vanity. And there might be at least a grain of truth in the accusation, though he knew himself to be perilously unfit for the role of knight-errant at the moment. As this morning had shown so disastrously.

But at least no one could accuse him of idealizing the object of his romantic intentions. So far he had seen Cat shabby, untidy, and even attired in her brother's breeches; and she had been alternately angry, defiant, and even icily contemptuous in his presence. She had done nothing to attract his attention and a great deal to drive him away.

And yet none of it seemed to matter, for her face and personality were vibrantly alive in his memory, when all the other milk-and-water misses he had met in London had somehow merged into one another, so that he found he could not recall a single one of their faces at the moment.

Certainly he need never worry that Cat would run that risk. If he succeeded in winning her, she would doubtless be annoying, opinionated, and fiercely independent. She was beautiful in a way she seemed wholly unconscious of, and could hold her own in any society without fear of comparison. But he did not deceive himself that she would make a conformable wife or that her background, to say nothing of her grandfather, was likely to find favor with his family.

Even that did not deter him, however, which told him how far gone he was. He cared a little for his family's opinion, but he certainly did not mean to allow it to change his mind. He supposed, if he had ever bothered to consider the matter at all, that he had always assumed he would marry a quiet, well-bred lady, someone of his world who was acceptable to his parents. But he had never had any intention of allowing them to dictate that choice to him.

And one look at Cat was all it had taken to make him abandon without regret any vague, uneventful vision of his future he might have cherished. If Cat would have him, they would fight and love and work together to build something

they could be proud of. If not . . . But then, that did not bear
thinking of. It was too near reality for comfort.

He discovered he was frowning and that a fresh-faced,
oddly familiar youth was regarding him rather shyly from
across the road. The youth had stopped to gaze into a
milliner's window, but as the major looked up, he hesitated,
then determinedly crossed the road to meet him.

At the moment, the last thing the major wanted was
company, but he stopped, waiting for the youth to join him.
He supposed he must be the son of some friend, or someone
he had met in London, but for the moment he could not place
his face.

Then, as the youth reached him and smiled shyly at him,
with a hint of his sister's elusive grace, Simon recognized
who he must be.

"Are you . . . ? That is, you must be Lord Simon," the
youth said ingenuously. "I've been wanting to meet you,
sir, and never more than after this morning. I'm Jamie
Dunraven, Cat's brother, you know."

Simon didn't know quite what he had expected, but not
this boy with the open face and confiding manner. It was
obvious that he was younger than Cat, and had none of her
dark depths. In fact it was easy to see that he would be no
match for his older sister.

In all other respects, however, he bore a strong resemblance to her, with the same black hair, startlingly blue eyes,
and cleft chin.

Simon shook the boy's outstretched hand, wondering if
he were to be treated to Cat's hostility or their grandfather's
bland urbanity.

He soon saw it was neither, for the youth said eagerly,
"I say, have you got a moment? I've been wanting a chance
to talk to you ever since Cat told me . . . that is, ever since
I heard who you were. And I especially wanted to thank you

for your interference this morning. Could we go and get a drink or something?''

The major was in strong need of an ally at the moment, and so did not hesitate to accept this invitation. He suspected Cat would be furious when she came to hear of it, but squelched that problem for the moment.

The youth seemed equally oblivious of the danger. He turned to walk eagerly beside him, carefully keeping his eyes from the major's stiff leg, though his color was a little high.

Simon felt oddly reassured by Jamie's obvious normality. He had had dozens of just such fresh-faced youths under him, and understood them well. Jamie seemed to have a good deal of his grandfather's charm, but without his guile, and almost wholly lacked his sister's mistrust. In fact, if anything, he seemed too trusting.

The major was quickly to realize how much young Jamie had in common with the army-mad young subalterns under him, for as they went along, the youth added guilelessly, ''As a matter of fact, one of the reasons I particularly wanted to meet you—before today, that is—is that I would love to hear about your military career, sir, if you wouldn't find it too tedious. Chicklade told me you were at Ciudad Rodrigo, and, well . . . I've read everything I can find about it, and all the dispatches, but of course that's hardly like being there, is it?''

''Very unlike, I should imagine,'' said the major in some amusement. ''But you'd find it very dull hearing, I'm afraid. My memories of the battle are necessarily hazy.''

The youth colored, as if he were guilty of a solecism. ''Of course. But that wouldn't matter! I . . . well, I once had an ambition to join the army myself. It . . . it came to nothing in the end, but . . . well, I'd count it as a favor to hear whatever you'd care to tell me.''

The major recognized all the signs of just such an army-mad youth as he himself had once been, and felt a reluctant sympathy. "I'd be happy to, but I must confess it would seem your life is exciting enough already. Your grandfather and your sister certainly seem to find racing all they need."

The youth hunched a thin shoulder and looked vaguely embarrassed for some reason. "Oh, *Cat!* It's all right for her. I sometimes think she must have been born on the back of a horse. Not that I don't love horses myself, but . . . well, it's not quite the honorable sport most people think it."

Then he grinned and shrugged. "At any rate, I daresay you always despise what you've been raised around."

"Yes, I daresay. I was always secretly relieved I didn't have to step into my father's august shoes," agreed the major sympathetically. "But if you mean it, why did you give up on your military ambitions?"

They had reached the taproom of the major's inn by this time, and the youth self-consciously looked away as the major awkwardly climbed the shallow steps to the front door. "Oh, I don't know," he said vaguely. "I couldn't leave Cat . . . At any rate, it was only ever a dream. I was born to this life, as Sir James frequently points out. What will you have to drink, sir?"

They settled at a table. Lord Simon discreetly managing to pay for the beer they ordered. He wondered at the same time what had become of their mother and father. It seemed that both brother and sister called their grandfather "Sir James," as if he were a mere acquaintance.

As the waiter brought their beers, glancing curiously at them as he did so, his lordship idly asked the question: "Where are your parents, if you don't mind my asking?"

"Oh, Mother died when I was five, and Dad was killed ten years ago in a steeplechase. I remember him pretty well, but Cat's three years older than I am, so she remembers more, of course."

"You have always lived with your grandfather, then?"

The youth frowned. "Yes. That is, Mother took us both back to Ireland with her once." Then he grinned unselfconsciously. "It seems she was of respectable Irish stock and didn't approve of Sir James very much. But, well, Dad talked her into coming back—the Dunravens have always had more then their fair share of charm, I fear—and she died not long after. Cat remembers her well. It's one of the reasons . . . Well, never mind. But she and Sir James don't always get along, as you obviously already know. And I've always thought that was probably one of the reasons."

The major longed to pump this absurdly confiding boy, but some sense of honor, and Cat's almost undoubted contempt, kept him from taking advantage of the situation as he would have liked to. Ethics sometimes had their drawbacks.

So he deftly switched the subject to military matters, knowing that Jamie would eagerly follow his lead. He seldom cared to talk of that part of his life now, but he entertained the boy with some amusing anecdotes of military life.

Jamie drank it in, wide-eyed, belying his earlier assertion that he had give up his military ambitions. His obvious enjoyment and wistful questions made the major feel slightly guilty, wondering if he was doing him any favors by encouraging an interest that was obviously out of the question for some reason. But it seemed the safest topic.

Then Jamie said abruptly, flushing a little, "I . . . But I haven't thanked you yet for . . . well, for protecting Cat this morning, which is really what I wanted to talk to you about."

"Who told you I did?" the major asked curiously.

"Chicklade. He . . . I . . . I don't know what to do, sir," he burst out. "Cat doesn't take me seriously, and Sir James . . . well, Sir James is Sir James. But Baggett is dangerous. And he means no good to my sister.''

"He told me he meant to marry her.''

"Yes, but . . . Good God, sir! Surely you can see she's above . . . Oh, God, what's the use?'' he said drearily. "I should find some way of rescuing her, but I confess I don't see how. And now she's got this harebrained—'' Abruptly he stopped and colored deeply before finishing hastily. "I . . . Never mind. I forgot what I was going to say.''

His lordship decided his ethics would just have to be jettisoned for once. "What does Baggett have over your sister?'' he asked bluntly.

But Jamie had belatedly remembered his loyalty, and had colored even more. "I'm sorry, sir,'' he mumbled. "I should never have said anything. Cat would never forgive me if I . . . at any rate, you can't do anything, even if you wanted to. It's our problem.''

The major reluctantly did not press him, knowing that he would only lose Jamie's trust completely. But as he saw him off the premises with a promise to come soon and take potluck with them at the Downs, he wondered resignedly if he was ever going to make headway with any of the Dunravens.

11

The major found Cat giving his horse a workout the next morning when he drove over to the Downs.

She was in the same faded habit, and stood in the center of one of the far paddocks while the bay circled around her. Young Jem Chicklade was up on Conqueror's back, but he merely crouched there, the horse controlled by a long lead rein in Cat's hands.

As Simon watched, fascinated, she took the horse around and around the ring, forcing him to jump low gates and always keep to a steady canter, despite the bay's obvious desire to vary the pace. But unlike the bay, who seethed with impatience and frustration, Cat's patience seemed inexhaustible. As did her stamina, for it was grueling work in the hot sun.

After another twenty minutes she finally pulled the bay up and signaled to Jem to cool him down. As she wiped her own face with a handkerchief, she at last glanced over toward Simon. She hesitated almost visibly, then reluctantly walked over to where he stood leaning on the paddock fence.

He smiled warmly at her and wondered how it was she always managed to look so beautiful under conditions that would horrify other women. Her hair was tumbling down, her face was streaked with dust, and her shabby habit and gloves were coated with it. "I had no idea training a racing horse was so exhausting," he said frankly.

For her part, Cat had been aware of his lordship's presence almost from the moment he appeared. But she had steadfastly refused to give in to the temptation to look in his direction. It was vital not to lose concentration when working with a horse, and her hands and voice had never faltered, though she felt his eyes on her the whole time.

Now she took in his easy elegance and immaculate state and retorted somewhat snappishly, "Few owners do. But it's more boring than exhausting—for both of us. We'd both rather be doing something else."

"Why do you do it, then?"

She looked for some hint of condescension, but he sounded genuinely interested. Some of her stiffness deserted her, and she answered more readily, "Few racehorses like to work. They like to run, but that's not the same thing as winning. Conqueror, here, is relatively fast, but he has none of the discipline a racehorse needs. He expends all his energy on fighting everything that crosses his path, from the groom who saddles him to the jockey on his back, to other horses, when he should be concentrating on running."

He looked amused at this insight into equine thought processes. "I begin to see why your grandfather says you witch horses. Do you always get inside their heads?"

She shrugged. "Any good trainer does that. A great horse has to have not only the speed and the discipline to win but also the desire to win. That sounds ridiculous, I know, but I've seen horses literally burst their hearts to win, or run on an injury until they destroy themselves. No reputable trainer or jockey should allow that, of course, but it happens. A champion racehorse knows nothing about purses. He only knows that he can't let any other horse pass him by."

"You say 'he.' But surely there have been a few great fillies?"

"A few. By and large the female of any species lacks the killer instinct. I said the will to win made a great horse, not a smart one."

He burst out laughing. "I can see I have a lot to learn."

She turned abruptly to walk toward the stable block, knowing he would either have to remain where he was or put himself at the disadvantage of betraying his limp. She expected him to be annoyed by her tactic, but he merely strolled somewhat awkwardly beside her, unaware of or ignoring his handicap.

She saw that he seemed to be leaning more heavily on his stick that morning than usual, and that reminded her of something she would sooner forget.

But she made it a point always to pay her debts, and so she said stiltedly, "I believe I haven't yet thanked you for your help yesterday. It was unnecessary, but you obviously didn't know that."

Even in her own ears she sounded churlish, but he merely said cheerfully, "If it was unnecessary, then no thanks are needed. They wouldn't be in any case. I only did what any other man would have done."

She stopped, a bitter and foolish honesty not allowing her to let that pass. "In point of fact, few men would have done it, especially in—" She broke off, her eyes going involuntarily to his face. But she saw only amusement and something else there—something much warmer, not the anger she had been expecting.

"I'm sorry!" she said stiffly. "In your presence I seem to forget what few manners I possess."

"Don't apologize. One of the things I first . . . liked about you was that you didn't ignore my handicap or pretend it didn't exist, as so many of my well-meaning friends do.

Obviously it's a fact of life I must adjust to. At any rate, I think you know by now that I was not exactly a . . . disinterested party yesterday. So my unnecessary interference, as you called it, was hardly altruistic.''

So it had come. She found it suddenly hard to breathe, though she had long since recovered from her earlier exertion. She had known already that he wanted her, so his words should have come as no surprise. But for the first time in her life she could not dismiss the situation with her usual contempt. For whatever reason, she was tempted, and that terrified her.

At last she managed to say evenly enough, "And you . . . expect some kind of reward?"

"Reward? That's an odd way of putting it, but I suppose I do." They both had forgotten they stood in the middle of a field, and had forgotten about returning to the stable block. He hesitated and added simply, "I had no intention of blurting out that absurd proposal the other morning on the heath, but only because the timing was obviously wrong. I meant every word of it. I would count it a . . . great honor if you would consent to be my wife."

Cat had thought she was beyond being shocked by anything, but he had managed to prove her wrong. She was trembling for some reason, and her hands felt cold and her cheeks, by contrast, hot and flushed. "You must be mad," she whispered, her eyes huge in her suddenly pale face. "Either that or still suffering from a recurring fever."

He laughed out loud. "I assure you I'm neither. You must know how beautiful you are, and I can't believe I'm the first man to . . . admire you."

"They usually don't offer marriage, though," she pointed out, deliberately trying to shock him.

Then something in his very silence made her look up, and she immediately regretted it, for she surprised such a look of anger on his face that she was once more badly shaken.

"I begin to see why you . . . are the way you are. And I have never quite despised my own class so much as now," he said quietly.

For some reason she found herself wanting to protect him from the bitter reality of the world, and the absurd impulse angered her. "Oh, it isn't only your class," she said cynically. "It seems neither my background nor my life to date has fitted me for respectability. Since I was old enough to walk, I've been the intimate of double dealers of every stripe, from legs to Captain Hackums, from touts to mouths and demi-beaus and park saunterers. Or hasn't it yet occurred to you that you might find it a trifle embarrassing to introduce me to the world as your wife?"

"What has occurred to me, my sweet Cat, is that you underrate yourself shockingly," he said, his eyes steady on hers. "Any man would be proud to call you his wife."

She laughed, though there was nothing but bitterness in the sound. "Aye, so proud I have received exactly one offer of marriage in my life, and 'honorable' is the last word I would apply to it. But then, I fear that even I don't know which of the colorful tales of his origins my grandfather likes to tell is the true one, or even if he has any actual claim to the fine-sounding name of Dunraven that he likes to emblazon on everything he touches. A fine bride for Lord Simon Grey, youngest son of the Duke of Salford! Whenever your father attended Newmarket, I could point out all my old cronies to him, along with those my grandfather has cheated!"

He was himself a little pale by that time. "Good God, do you think any of that matters to me, you little fool? Or that I could reach the age of three-and-thirty without knowing my own mind? How the devil do you think I managed to remain single until now, if that were the case? Don't make me appear a complete coxcomb by boasting to you of the lures I've resisted until now."

She turned away abruptly, knowing it must be true. Even

without his birth and wealth he would be the object of feminine competition, because he represented everything a woman could hope for in a husband. The thought of those expensive, beautiful women had her fingers curling into claws despite herself.

"I think," she said in a low voice, "that for some reason you have chosen to think me . . . I can't imagine *what* it is you think me, for God knows I've given you little enough reason to like me. But if you are imagining me some sort of gallant figure, worthy of rescue, nothing could be further from the truth. You are at loose ends, and . . . and looking for some dragon to slay, perhaps. But I am no princess imprisoned in a tower. I fear I long ago lost any innocence or illusions I might have had."

She was tempted then to tell him the truth, for that would be the simplest and safest way of driving him away for good. But some scrap of pride—and self-preservation—prevented her from taking so irrevocable a step. Abruptly she hardened her voice and turned back. "So you see, I am in no need of rescuing, for the truth is, my grandfather and I are a great deal alike," she said defiantly. "This is the life I'm suited to, and none other. And I desire neither your pity nor your condescension."

"If that is intended to drive me away, I'm araid it has failed," he answered steadily. "My friends would tell you that I never resist a challenge, and you have provided me with the greatest challenge I've ever encountered. So be warned, Miss Dunraven. I have somewhat of a reputation for finishing what I start. And for getting what I want."

When Cat came down to dinner later that evening, Jamie was already there before her. Dinner was the one meal Sir James insisted they dress for—especially since the rest were taken on the run, or missed completely half the time—so she was in an old evening gown that had seen better days.

Jamie rose as she entered, and threw aside the newspaper he had been reading. He managed most of the business side of the stables and ran errands and handled the contacts with the other owners and trainers, and Cat knew she would have had difficulty managing without him. But she knew Jamie chafed under the tedium of his role.

He was good-natured enough to seldom show it, however, and tonight he reported on various commissions she had given him that morning. "Incidentally," he added with a grin, "old Grangely is suddenly more than willing to supply us feed on the same terms he refused last month. It appears the news of our wealthy new client has had unexpectedly positive results. The old skinflint swore two weeks ago he'd not let us have another bag on tick. This time he practically fawned on me, inviting me to eat my mutton there whenever I chose and not to stand on ceremony. He asked after you as well. Said his wife had been meaning to pay you a call."

Cat had thrown herself down on a chair with little concern for ladylike graces. "Aye, to gather gossip about his lordship, no doubt," she said cynically. Their neighbor boasted little pretensions to gentility, but his wife had seldom condescended to notice either Cat or Jamie, considering them socially beneath her. She was intensely ambitious, however, and now was obviously willing to overlook their flaws in the interests of cultivating an introduction to the area's newest celebrity.

Newmarket was used to important visitors, but even in such a place Lord Simon Grey must occasion flattering notice. Cat wondered if the few upper-class families had already contrived to lay claim to him.

Well, they were welcome to him. He would find the Misses Grangely little to his taste, for they resembled their sandy-haired papa; but there were several charming daughters in the vicinity who were likely to appeal to him. At any rate, whether or not he was interested, he would find it difficult to decline their mamas' insistent hospitality, for such a noted matrimonial prize was not easily to be overlooked. Cat told herself she was glad he would at least be well-entertained during his stay in Newmarket.

As if somehow reading her thoughts, Jamie said hesitantly, "I met Lord Simon the other day in town, you know. And I liked him."

Cat closed her eyes, for she hardly had any need to be told the latter, at least. Jamie liked everyone, and it was a foregone conclusion that he would develop an instant hero worship for someone who was not only the eptiome of a gentleman but also a military hero.

But since she had no wish to discuss the subject of Lord Simon, least of all with her brother, she said merely, in a bored voice, "Did you? Before I forget, did you remember to call in and see if the new supply of spermaceti oil is in yet? One of the horses seems to be developing a shin splint."

But she should have known Jamie was not so easily side-tracked. He answered her question, then added with something of puzzlement in his face, "By the way, did you know Lord Simon's horse is attracting almost as much attention as he is? You haven't done any talking about him, have you?"

That brought her wide-awake, from the half-stupor she had fallen into. "No, I haven't," she said grimly. "But I'd be willing to wager a handsome fortune who has. I noticed that rascal Patch has been conspicuously absent from sight the last couple of days. He and Sir James are no doubt behind it."

When Jamie looked surprised, she added bitterly, "I take it his lordship didn't inform you, during this cozy little chat of yours, that Sir James had talked into him entering Conqueror in the Two Thousand Guineas."

Jamie looked shocked. "Good lord! Well, you thought he was up to something. What do you mean to do?"

"What can I do?"

He did not quite meet her eyes, but she noticed he was careful to keep his voice carefully neutral. "You mean to go through with it, then?"

She laughed without humor. "I'm sorry if it shocks you, but what choice have I? Sir James always said we were two of a kind, and it seems he was more right than I knew. It might also interest you to know that according to Patch, Baggett means to bring in a ringer."

Jamie's eyes widened. "Good Lord! I thought Philanderer was his pride and joy. I begin to see Sir James's game now. But dammit, I like his lordship, Cat. I . . . well, I don't want to see him made a fool of. Or worse."

Abruptly she turned on him with all her own pent-up frustration. "So what do you suggest? That we give up without a struggle and lose everything? You know I did all I could to keep him from coming here in the first place. If he's hurt, he has only himself to blame!"

"I don't like to see you so hard, Cat," said Jamie in a low, troubled voice.

She laughed a little wildly again. "You and Sir James should get together. He's afraid I'm growing too soft! All I know is that I can't lose the Downs. I can't!"

He frowned at her sudden vehemence. "I know Grandfather would be shattered, but why, Cat? To be honest, I never really thought you cared for it overmuch."

"I sometimes think I hate it!"

Then she was sorry for the outburst, for Jamie looked profoundly shocked. "Never mind. I don't really mean it," she said wearily. "But even if I did, what else am I to do? It's different for you. You can make your own way in the world, and should. But the only thing I can do if we lose the Downs is marry. And I have resisted selling myself this long. I don't want to be reduced to it in the end."

110   *Dawn Lindsey*

"You don't mean to marry Baggett, then?" Jamie asked in some relief.

"I don't know what I mean. If I did, you could at least have your dream. I know you only stay because of me. I sometimes think I'm selfish for not marrying him. But I can't . . . Oh, God, never mind. You must know I'm just blue-deviled this evening."

Jamie was looking troubled, for it was unlike her to unburden herself so frankly. She made herself lift her head and make an attempt to throw off her unaccustomed depression. "I'm sorry, Jamie, I'm just tired. And hungry. Let's hope Brigid hasn't ruined dinner yet again. Somehow it would be the last straw."

12

The major drove back to Newmarket in a thoughtful mood.

He was ruefully aware he had not shown to advantage in the last couple of days, and had never cursed his handicap more. But at least he had gotten through Cat's powerful defenses to some degree, for she was no longer merely icily indifferent in his presence. He supposed for the moment he must be content with even that small amount of progress.

But he had been angered and somewhat chastened by her revelations of what her life must be like. He wanted to lift all the burdens from her shoulders and protect her from the world. Unfortunately, at the moment he didn't even have the right to deal with Baggett as he longed to.

He had learned enough about the man in the past few days to add greatly to his concern. It seemed Baggett was unpopular in the district, but endured for his wealth and undoubted power. He was widely believed to have his hand in any number of shady operations, and also owned the odds-on favorite in the Two Thousand Guineas race that Simon's own horse was to enter.

It was not difficult to guess that he had some hold over Cat or her grandfather. But without knowing what it was, or having the right to confront Baggett on Cat's behalf, Simon's hands seemed to be effectively tied.

He swore, thinking he had never felt so helpless—or so frustrated. So long as Cat continued to hold him at arm's length, there seemed precious little he could do. He hoped he had at least put a stop to those dangerous solitary rides, for he was a shrewd judge of character, and he felt instinctively that Chicklade could be trusted. It was obvious he was devoted to her, and Simon would just have to rely upon him to do what he could to protect her.

Unfortunately, Chicklade couldn't be everywhere at once, and it seemed to Simon that Cat was constantly vulnerable— as that scene with Baggett had demonstrated all too clearly. She seemed to take for granted a high degree of freedom for one of her sex, and it was easy to see why. So far as he had yet been able to tell, she was involved in every aspect of the running of the stables, and seemed to work from sunup to sundown.

Which brought him to yet another unpleasant truth. He longed to protect her from every ill wind, but in point of fact, so far all it seemed he had managed to do was add significantly to her burdens. Certainly before coming to Newmarket he had never considered that she might have had a valid reason for not wishing to take on his horse. Used to his father's highly efficient organization, which teemed with grooms and ostlers and exercise boys, he had never before realized that horse training could entail so much hard work—all of which seemed to fall directly on Cat's slender shoulders.

Jamie was obviously willing to help her, but it was easy to see he lacked her driving will. And Chicklade was quietly protective, but Cat seemed to be the driving force behind everything.

The obvious solution, of course, would have been to give

up and do as she obviously wanted, by withdrawing his horse. But he was reluctant to do so on several counts. Not only did he suspect she needed the money, but it certainly would deprive him of any excuse to visit the Downs. And he was not yet sure enough of her to risk that.

Unfortunately, now that he was familiar with Cat's stubborn pride, the only other obvious answer seemed to be equally untenable. He could, of course, offer to pay for any extra help necessitated by the presence of his horse. But he suspected that that logical solution was unlikely to meet with anything but scorn from Cat.

So for the present it seemed he could do little but bide his time and keep his eyes and ears open—a practice in no way suited to his active temperament. If Cat had presented him with more than enough challenge to banish his recent boredom, he still would have preferred something more concrete to do—something he could sink his teeth into. The days in camp just before a battle had always been his least favorite time.

He had taken to leaving Aikins behind when he drove to the Downs, suspecting that his henchman was far from approving of this latest escapade. But the major was not surprised to find the groom lingering in the inn yard waiting for him when he at last drove up. There was an expression of anxiety on the groom's weather-beaten face that he instantly tried to banish as he went to the horses' heads.

"Has the bay settled in all right, my lord?" he asked conversationally.

"It would appear so. I found Miss Dunraven working him when I arrived, and he seemed to have reformed overnight." Simon climbed awkwardly down from the curricle and added with a grin. "She says he's fast enough but seems to lack the killer instinct that a winner needs."

Aikins was busy throwing a blanket over the leader, but

he, too, grinned at that. "If so, it wasn't so's I would notice on the drive down here. I must admit."

He went to throw a blanket on the other horse, and added, as if casually, "But if that's what it takes to make a winner, I'd say that black of Miss Dunraven's should certainly qualify. I've been hearing tales of him around town, and it seems he's notorious. He's said to have already killed at least one man afore. In fact, they all call 'im Cat's Folly."

The major's amusement instantly faded. "Good God! Are you sure?"

At the groom's nod he let out his breath in angry frustration. "Damnation! I'd like to know what the hell they think they're doing, letting her ride him in that case, without even a groom to accompany her. In fact, I must confess I'm fast losing what little tolerance I might have possessed for Sir James Dunraven."

"Word is in town that Miss Dunraven does pretty much as she likes," pointed out Aikins dryly.

"Then it's more than time she was stopped." Abruptly the major took in his groom's guarded expression, and added shortly, "And you can stop being so damned discreet. You obviously think I've landed myself in the worst coil yet, don't you?"

The groom seemed to have suddenly become overly interested in examining one of the chestnut's shoes. "I wouldn't say that, my lord," he answered without emotion. "Nor I've never known you to care one way or another what anyone thinks, once your mind was made up."

"And I don't now! But you can stop 'my-lording' me with every breath. I can always tell when I'm in your black books, since you start throwing my title at me every other sentence. You may as well get it off your chest. You think I'm making a fool of myself, don't you?"

The groom's dignity had thawed somewhat by then, but

he said merely, "I'm sure I don't know what your lordship is talking about."

"Damn you, Bob!"

Aikins' countenance softened even more. "Very well, my lord," he said grudgingly at last. "I have nothing against Miss Dunraven, of course. But I confess her grandfather's another matter. I've been keeping my ear to the ground since we arrived, and . . . well, he's none too savory a reputation here. In fact, it seems that if there's any skulduggery afoot, you can count that he'll be in on it in some way."

"And you think the fruit doesn't fall too far from the tree, is that it?" inquired the major with a flickering smile. He shrugged and added simply, "I have no proof to offer you that that isn't so, of course. Except my instincts, for what they're worth. And every instinct I possess tells me . . . *Good God!*" he suddenly exclaimed, breaking off. "Aikins, I must be the king of all fools! In fact, if I were still in the army, I should be cashiered for the sort of muddleheaded thinking the rawest recruit is guilty of. Of course! *Her grandfather!* Dammit, I've had the solution staring me straight in the face all along, only I was too blind to see it."

Aikins looked alert, as if expecting danger for some reason, but remained tactfully silent. After a moment the major wearily rubbed his tired neck. "In fact, I should go back and talk to him now, except that I can't yet face the thought of that long drive again. What I need is a hot bath and a glass of brandy, not necessarily in that order. I'll have to talk to Sir James in the morning."

Aikins, who had thought his master was looking tired and dispirited, instantly abandoned any effort to convince him of his folly in trusting so unknown a quantity as Miss Dunraven. "Duggans has already ordered it, Major. But now that I recall, I think you'll find something that will put the heart into you even better. It's waiting in your room."

The major regarded his servant in affectionate exasperation. "I'm not a seven-year-old boy to be cosseted out of my tantrums, you fool."

He started to say something more, then shrugged and climbed somewhat stiffly to his room, his groom's over-protectiveness already forgotten. He was stiff and in considerable pain after the last few active days, but he was scarcely aware of his own discomforts. He was tempted even yet to ride back to the Downs, for he could not dismiss the feeling that something was seriously wrong there.

He told himself he was being unnecessarily worried, and that nothing could happen in the next twenty-four hours. But he was still looking preoccupied when he entered the private parlor he had hired and went to pour himself a stiff glass of brandy.

"So there you are," complained a voice from behind him. "I'd begun to think you'd disappeared off the face of the earth, especially after the way Aikins and that long-faced niffy-naffy valet you've acquired since last I saw you were taking on. What the devil have you been up to to put them both in such a taking, by the way? I thought civilian life was going to reform you."

The major whirled, his expression incredulous. "*Jack!*" His face broke into a broad grin. "Jack, by all that's holy! Where the devil did you spring from? I thought you were still in Spain."

Major the Honorable John Robinette rose and gripped his friend's hand with a momentarily betraying pressure, before once more assuming his customary pose of lighthearted insouciance. "I might ask the same of you!" he retorted disrespectfully. "I expected you to still be at Salford recovering from your wounds, or at best in London, taking advantage of your limp to make yourself look interesting.

I couldn't believe my ears when I discovered you were holed up here for some reason. In fact, the general consensus in town seems to be that the fever has permanently addled your brain.''

He looked his friend over critically, and added, ''But I must say you're looking remarkably fit. I expected, after the last time I saw you in that so-called hospital in Lisbon, to find you still only half-alive. In fact, I hope never to see anyone looking more like a human scarecrow. I can only say civilian life must agree with you better than I thought it would.''

The major found himself more pleased than he liked to acknowledge at the sight of such an old friend. ''Never mind that now. Tell me what you're doing here. I don't mean New-market, you fool, but England. You haven't sold out, have you?''

As he spoke, he handed Major Robinette a glass of brandy and went to sink gratefully into a deep chair before the fire. Jack saluted him with a grin and downed half of his drink at one swallow before acknowledging. ''I've already tasted your brandy, I must confess, for I was getting devilish bored sitting here waiting for you. No, I haven't sold out. But I had some urgent business to attend to in connection with my brother's estate—the devil take all lawyers, by the way! The damned thing's been dragging on for almost a year now, and no nearer to a solution, from anything I can tell. But anyway, since we were enjoying something of a hiatus after the recent stirring events, I decided to come home and see if I couldn't wind it up more easily in person. Wellington—or I *should* say his lordship, of course! . . . an earldom and K.B.'s for Graham and Hill! . . . we *are* getting grand!—gave me two months, but if things heat up as I expect, I may be needed before then. But for the moment I'm enjoying a taste of civilization again and finding it damned hard to remember why I left in the first place. Especially after this last siege. You were lucky to have missed it.''

Simon sobered. "Yes. The newspaper accounts of Badajoz made it sound bad enough, sketchy as they were, but Oursdley and Denehy both wrote assuring me that it made even the taking of Rodrigo look pleasant by comparison.''

"They were right. The weather was damnable, which didn't help—but then, it always is before Wellington's battles. But I'll admit I've never seen anything to equal the slaughter. Time after time we tried to storm the breaches, across a damned deadly *chevaux-de-frise* defended by such heavy rifle fire it decimated any column that tried to remove it. So many officers had fallen that there were scarcely enough left to rally the troops. I must admit even I was beginning to think all was lost. But then, sometime after midnight, word came that Picton had taken the castle, and that seemed to turn the tide. But I thank God I wasn't in charge that night, for I'm not sure I would have counted the victory worth the cost.''

They reminisced for a good deal longer, until the shadows lengthened and they were at last reminded of the time by the arrival of the waiter bringing in the covers for dinner.

Simon roused himself then, and said abruptly, "Aside from every other reason, I'm damned glad to see you, as it happens, Jack. How long can you stay?''

Major Robinette paused, the ghost of a smile touching his mobile mouth. "Yes, I guessed you were in some sort of scrape. Not only from the cautious way Aikins was answering my questions, but by your face when you came in. I should have known you couldn't remain out of trouble. Of course I'll stay as long as you need me—but only on the condition you tell me everything. I won't soon forget the time you talked me into going on that mission with you when we were both nearly skewered by a French patrol. It was only afterward that I learned it was all in aid of one of your quixotic quests and I'd risked my neck for nothing.''

But as if by common consent, the subject was not broached again until after they had enjoyed an excellent meal. Once the covers had been removed, the candles trimmed, and the fire made up by an ever-attentive Duggans, and a bottle of port placed on the table between them, did Major Robinette sigh and comment half-jokingly, "Ah, this is the life. In fact, I'm damned if I can see what trouble you can find to get into in so tame a place."

"Not so tame as it would appear," said Simon seriously, and without hesitation launched into a brief description of what he had found at the Downs. He was well aware that beneath his flippant facade Jack was both a shrewd officer and a judge of men, and he had always valued his advice in the past.

"And the devil of it is, she won't do anything to make it any easier for me," he finished bitterly. "Aikins clearly thinks I've taken leave of my senses at a long last. But I can't help feeling . . . Dammit, it's more than that! I *know* my intuition is right about her. But whether or not it is, I only know she's the only woman for me."

His friend was looking unnaturally grave, but he knew better than to voice any of his natural misgivings. "Well, much as it pains me to admit it, I've seldom known your intuition to be wrong," he answered lightly. "It's certainly saved my life often enough—though usually you were the one to have risked it in the first place, I might add. But I can't help pointing out that regardless of whether you're right or wrong about this Miss Dunraven of yours, she seems to have made it pretty clear that she doesn't want you involved. You can hardly force her to marry you or to accept your help if she doesn't want it, you know."

Jack was prepared for Simon to be angry at this reasonable

reminder. He was not prepared for the slow lightening of
his old friend's expression, or the almost triumphant smile
that escaped him. "Can't I?" He laughed.

Then as Robinette gaped at him, he added softly, "And
I'm afraid you're right. It's beginning to look as if I won't
get her else."

13

Major Robinette rose late the next morning after a somewhat sleepless night, and sauntered to his friend's room, still wrapped in his colorful dressing gown. To his surprise, he found the room empty and its occupant evidently long gone.

He frowned and went back to dress, more concerned about Simon's bizarre tale of the night before than he liked to admit.

Admittedly he had known Simon to tumble in and out of any number of scrapes over the years, until it had become something of a standing joke in the regiment. Simon had always been a romantic, falling for every lame-duck or hard-luck story that came his way—and in time of war, there were inclined to be many. But Major Robinette had never before known him to fall in love with one of his protégées.

Oh, like the rest of them, he had pursued any number of dusky Spanish beauties and engaged in certain more or less irregular connections; but his heart had always seemed to remain untouched. There were always a few officers in the regiment who fell in love as regularly as clockwork and were always nursing a broken heart, but Simon certainly hadn't been one of them. It was almost as if he were waiting for something—it was probable that even he didn't know quite what—and would not settle for anything less.

But if some of Simon's friends had teased him about it now and then, they had none of them any suspicion that what he was waiting for would turn out to be an Irish beauty with a vulgar grandfather who was living in more than suspicious circumstances.

Nor was Simon's family likely to accept such a connection. In fact, they would probably have been less shocked if he had turned up with some Portuguese bride on his arm—at least if she had a spotless reputation and wealthy family.

In the regiment Simon might have been treated as just one of the fellows, and stood so little on his dignity that most tended to completely forget his august background. But the free and democratic give-and-take of a regiment in wartime was hardly the same as London society; nor were their graces likely to forget what was owed to their noble name. To accept into their family such a dubious bride would be out of the question, and Jack feared that his old friend had really landed himself in the suds this time.

But he was not the man to abandon a friend in need, and so after he had breakfasted he strolled out into the late-spring sunshine and wandered around to the stables.

There, as he had expected, he found Aikins polishing his lordship's saddle. The groom looked up and acknowledged his presence, but went on with his work.

Jack lounged at his ease and chatted mildly of the climate and the local scenery for a few moments. Only after some moments did he ask casually, "Lord Simon looks better than I'd expected, Aikins. How's he adjusting to everything?"

Both knew what he was asking. The groom put down the brush and answered somewhat briefly, "Well enough, sir. He was blue-deviled at first, o' course, but he's mostly over that."

"I'm glad to hear it. It's a miracle he's alive at all, though I feared at first he wouldn't think so. But he seems to be getting around well enough. They tell me he's even back in the saddle now. Just don't let him overdo it.''

The groom picked up his brush again and dipped it into the saddle soap, making no answer. After a moment Major Robinette said even more delicately, "I only know he looked half-dead the last time I saw him. I hear he suffered a good deal from fever. Er . . . ah . . . his mind seem all right now?''

Aikins looked up at that, a hint of amusement in his eyes. "His mind was never in any way affected, if that's what's worrying you, sir.''

"Good. Well, I . . . ah . . . guess I'll wander through town, then go for a drive later this morning. If his lordship gets back before I do, tell him that I'll see him at dinner.''

Simon had ridden out early, a taciturn Aikins by his side, then returned and driven straight back to the Downs.

He was a little reassured, for he had caught sight of Cat from a distance, mounted on her black; but this time a burly figure the major recognized as Chicklade was accompanying her. He wondered briefly how she had taken to the idea of an escort, but could only be glad Chicklade had been as good as his word.

The major found Sir James and Jamie still at a belated breakfast, and was conducted in by the slovenly and disapproving housemaid.

Jamie flushed a little and greeted him shyly, but Sir James welcomed him almost regally. The major was again unwillingly amused by the supreme confidence of the man he hoped soon would become his grandfather-in-law. But he had discovered a distinct limit to his tolerance, and was no longer much inclined to forgive him his many faults where Cat was concerned.

He accepted a cup of coffee, then said bluntly, before Sir

James could launch into one of his colorful tales, "I'm sorry to disturb you so early, sir, but I had something of a somewhat serious nature that I wanted to discuss with you."

Sir James looked only mildly surprised. "Anything, anything, me boy, you know that," he said expansively. "Which reminds me, Caity tells me that horse of yours is lookin' promisin'."

Simon refused to be sidetracked. "I'm glad to hear it, but as a matter of fact, it's your granddaughter I wanted to speak to you about. Did she tell you I found your neighbor Baggett forcing himself upon her the other day?"

Jamie looked acutely embarrassed, but Sir James merely frowned. "I've no liking for the man, God knows, but ye'll not tell me my Caity found it hard to deal with such a miserable spalpeen herself? She's twice the man he ever thought of being."

"She's no man at all, a fact you seem to have forgotten," replied his lordship, an unaccustomed edge to his voice. "As for dealing with him, you seem to possess some odd notion of the respective sizes of your granddaughter and Baggett. If I hadn't stumbled on the scene, I don't like to think what might have happened."

Sir James looked briefly irritated, but managed to cover the betraying emotion. "If so, it's grateful I am to ye, my lad, but I still suspect ye may have misunderstood the situation just a trifle. My Caity's not afraid of Baggett, nor of any man."

Simon found himself growing increasingly angry at such willful blindness, but forced himself to control his rising irritation. "I wish I might think so. But are you aware, by any chance, that Baggett is freely boasting all over town that he means to marry your granddaughter?"

"Over my dead body!" roared Sir James, moved at last

to indignation. "Caity knows I won't have that black-hearted divil in the family."

"I wonder why I don't find that a very useful attitude?" remarked his lordship with some grimness. "It might interest you to know that I have every reason to suspect your grand-daughter is extremely afraid of Baggett, although she denies it as well. I was hoping you would be able to tell me why."

Sir James began to bluster. "Even if she were—a notion which is laughable, I assure you—I'd like to know by what right ye come thrustin' yer nose into my granddaughter's affairs. Or perhaps it's escaped your notice that she has both a grandfather and a brother to protect her."

"No, it hasn't escaped my notice," retorted the major even more grimly. "I thought perhaps it had escaped yours. As for my right to interfere, I perhaps should inform you that I have every intention of marrying your granddaughter if she'll have me."

Jamie choked on his coffee and seemed to be overcome, and even Sir James seemed mildly startled. "Eh, so that's the way the wind lies, is it?" he said in amusement. "Well, I'm not surprised, for she's a beautiful lass. Still, so far as I was aware, it is customary, even in these degenerate times, to request her guardian's permission."

"That is exactly why I'm here. Have I your permission to pay my addresses to Miss Dunraven?" responded his lordship promptly.

Sir James settled back in his chair, in supreme command of himself. "As to that, I'm by no means certain ye have," he asserted outrageously. "I've no mind to give her to just anybody. Ye'd have to go far to find her equal, in looks *or* breeding. Just like her grandmother, she is. Aye, there was a queen among women. In fact, a duke might think himself lucky to have my Caity, and so I'll tell anyone."

"Grandfather!" cried Jamie, very red in the face.

But Simon was merely amused by this posing. "Why stop there?" he inquired politely. "If you're so ambitious, I believe there are still several royal princes available."

Sir James acknowledged it expansively. "Ye may laugh, but it's a rare queen she'd have made. Ye've obviously seen her beauty and courage for yourself. I have no hesitation in saying that there's not another in the kingdom to compare with her."

"I fully agree with you, sir. Unfortunately, I'm by no means certain your granddaughter does. I've no wish to offend you—since I have every hope you will be my grand-father-in-law before much longer—but you must know your granddaughter has taken the brunt of your . . . er . . . colorful reputation. I will also confess that while I would appreciate your blessing, the presence or absence of it will make no material difference to my intentions. In fact, I have already asked your granddaughter to marry me."

Sir James looked more than interested. "Have ye, now? And what did she say?"

"She refused me," Simon admitted. "And I think you know why."

"Ah, well, she's a mind of her own, has my Caity," said Sir James proudly. "And as hard to please in men as she is in horseflesh, it would appear. Ye've no need to take it to heart."

"*Grandfather!*" pleaded Jamie.

Simon had to discipline his wayward lips. "That may be, sir. But I think the reason has more to do with you than with me. And with whatever hold it is Baggett has over her."

If he had hoped to succeed by using shock tactics, he was to be disappointed. Sir James merely waved that away. "You may safely leave Baggett to me, my boy. I have every intention of taking care of him meself."

Simon had suddenly lost all desire to laugh. "May I?" he said hardly. "I wish I might believe that, sir. That's partly why I came, for as it stands, I have no right to confront Baggett myself. And your granddaughter refused to give me that right, out of a misguided sense of pride and loyalty, I suspect. But I give you fair warning: I will intervene if necessary. Nor will I hesitate to remove your granddaughter if I believe her to be in danger."

"Danger!" scoffed Sir James. "And what danger might she be in here, under the eye of her grandfather and brother?"

"Enough danger that your head groom feels the need to go armed. I also gather from Miss Dunraven that she has been subjected to more than Baggett's unwanted attentions. In fact, I don't scruple to tell you that her upbringing has been damnable. She has been made to feel an outcast all her life, owing to your background and behavior, and I must confess I can find little evidence of your so-called protection. But I didn't come here today to pick a bone with you."

"If not, ye're doing a damned fine job of it!" roared Sir James, much incensed. "I'm beginning to think Caity was in the right to refuse you, me lord! If ye've not the eyes to see that there's not another to match her for wits and beauty and spirit in the whole of this miserable damp country, whoever her grandfather may be, then ye're not worthy of her, and so I take leave to tell ye!"

"Stop it, Grandfather!" Jamie had been silent all that time in embarrassment, but now his voice sounded unexpectedly hard. "Everything Lord Simon says is true. I've known it for years, and you would too if you weren't too wrapped up in your own affairs to see what's under your nose. Cat has borne the brunt of everything, and I for one intend to see that it stops. Good God, haven't you ever wondered why she, with her wits and beauty as you call it, has received no other offer than from that fool Baggett? It's because of you, not to mention that she's run this stable almost single-handedly for years, and has had to mix with the worst sort of men, until the decent women in town won't receive her. And if she . . . that is, if Lord Simon is able to see past her circumstances to her true worth, then I for one will do everything I can to help him!''

"Thank you, Jamie," said his lordship more mildly. "But as I said, I really didn't come here today to cast stones. And without wishing to appear unduly immodest, I think I could manage to overcome Cat's objections if that were all it was. But it has been clear to me since I first arrived that she's deathly afraid of something. I was hoping your grandfather could tell me what that was.''

He eyed his future grandfather-in-law steadily, but Sir James had had a chance to recover himself. "Nonsense!" he said dismissively. "I will put your excesses down to the very natural concern of a man in love, my boy—and well for you I do, for I tell ye frankly that without my permission ye'll not have my Caity, were you ten times the son of a duke! But you may take my word for it that I have my own and my granddaughter's affairs well in hand. And now, good day to ye. I've one or two matters to attend to. No, don't get up! Stay and finish your coffee.''

As he strolled blithely out, the two remaining could only shake their heads at each other. "He's always like that, you know," Jamie said apologetically. "There's never getting anything out of him. Cat and I gave it up years ago."

Then he sobered. "I . . . Did you mean it about marrying Cat, sir?'' he asked diffidently. "Because, if so, I for one couldn't be happier. I think you're just the man for her, and I don't mean just because of your wealth and title. You may not believe it, sir, but Cat doesn't care about any of that either.''

Then abruptly his expression changed ludicrously. "Oh, Lord! I just remembered . . ."

But when Simon looked a question, he merely shook his head, though he looked suddenly pale. He soon found a reason to excuse himself as well, all his earlier confiding air completely gone.

The major frowned, but rose and followed him somewhat grimly, strolling slowly out to the stables. His suspicions that Jamie knew what was going on were now crystallized, but it was obvious that for some reason the boy had no intention of confiding in him. The major would have given a good deal at that moment to know what had occurred to the boy to shut him up so rapidly and turn him from a confiding youth to a silent stranger.

When the major got to the stableyard, he was surprised to find the place unexpectedly tense. Jamie had evidently preceded him, for he and the head groom and his son were all in close conversation, looking worried.

All three looked up as the major limped into view, and Jamie had the grace to blush a little.

"What's going on?" the major inquired mildly.

Chicklade hesitated, then, as if making up his mind to something, said deliberately, "That blasted black o' Miss Cat's has savaged one o' the undergrooms. But you needn't worry, my lord. He's kept nowhere near your horse."

The major felt his heart grow cold with fear for a brief moment, again seeing Cat on the brute's back as she had been that morning. "How badly is he hurt?" he demanded curtly.

"Broke his leg. He's lucky it wasn't his head. I'd warned the fool to stay away."

"That seems to be scant comfort at the moment," said the major. "In fact, I understand he's killed at least one man already. Hardly a suitable mount for a lady, I would have thought.''

A brief glint of humor showed in the groom's worried face. ''No doubt. But happen you've yet to realize no one never stopped Miss Cat once she'd taken a notion into her head.''

''Well, it seems to me that it's time someone did,'' replied the major with undue grimness, looking nothing like his usual pleasant self. ''Where is she?''

Something resembling respect flickered in the groom's eyes, but he merely jerked his head toward the nearest stable block. ''No doubt,'' he said again. ''But beggin' your pardon, Major, while I've no wish to call your military career into question, ye've yet to see Miss Cat in a temper, I'm thinkin'. Boney's soldiers ain't got nothing on her.''

The major laughed, his spirits rising at the thought of the confrontation ahead, and limped off in the direction of the stables.

14

Simon found Cat in one of the boxes, calmly engaged in the homely task of mucking it out.

Everything else was instantly wiped from his mind. "What the *devil* do you think you're doing?" he thundered.

Cat jumped, then stiffened as she realized who it was, and made no attempt to stop what she was doing. "What does it look like?" she returned flippantly.

"Give me that!" When she ignored him, the major forcibly took the pitchfork from her.

Her eyes flashed fire for a moment, but then she shrugged. "I'll just finish as soon as you've gone."

Simon fought the simultaneous desires to kiss away her sulky ill humor and to turn her over his knee, but managed to resist both of them. "I hadn't realized mucking out stables was also part of your duties. Surely someone else can be found to do such mundane tasks?"

"Unfortunately, this is not Salford, my lord. Nor am I nearly so proud as you. With Jenkins out, there is no one else."

Again he managed to cure his growing impatience. "If you're really that shorthanded, I'll send Aikins out this afternoon to help. And if that's why you didn't want to take on my horse, you little fool, you should have said so. Obviously it is my responsibility to pay for any extra staff that may be needed.''

Her brows rose. "And where do you propose we find this 'extra staff'?'' she demanded mockingly.

"Good God, how should I know? Surely there are any number of men hanging about in Newmarket who would like steady employment?''

"Undoubtedly. But if they have any experience, they've either been turned off from one of the other stables for incompetence or will have been sent to spy on us.''

"You can't be serious.''

She shrugged. "There's been a good deal of curiosity about you locally, and the son of the Duke of Salford represents a considerable threat. I've already had two men inquire about employment here and offer to work for less than the going wage. We'll do without extra help until Jenkins is back on his feet, if it's all the same to you.''

"But this is incredible!''

"I told you this was far from being a gentleman's sport,'' she reminded him. "There've been half a dozen horses poisoned in Newmarket alone in the last year. And that doesn't include the more mundane bribings and spying and usual dirty tricks that your sort prefers to close their eyes to.''

"Good God! And to think I was just lamenting the lack of excitement in civilian life. How old are you, by the way?'' he asked unexpectedly.

She looked startled, and for once uncertain. "I . . . twenty-three. Why?''

His face had softened. "Nothing. I just wondered. It seems very young to be so cynical.''

She gave a laugh that sounded almost like a sob. "That should tell you something about the difference between us. I am already older than you will ever be.''

"My dear . . . what is it?" he inquired gently.

She gave a shuddering breath and turned away. "Oh, God, go back to London where you belong! This is no place for you. Leave . . . leave your horse if you must. I promise I'll look after it. But go now—before it's too late."

"Sweetheart—"

She leaned her head back and shook it, as if it were suddenly too heavy for her slender neck. "Oh, God . . ." she whispered, "I'm so afraid . . ."

When she broke off and didn't finish, he said quietly, "That has been apparent to me for some time."

She turned back then. "Not for myself!" she cried contemptuously. "I can take care of myself. I was bred to this sort of life. You weren't."

He thought he had never been so touched as by this unexpected and somewhat naive concern. "Sweetheart, surely you can't really believe me quite so innocent. I was an officer of the line for more than ten years, remember."

"I sometimes think even war must be civilized by comparison with this. At any rate, that was before you . . ."

She broke off, coloring, and he finished for her cheerfully enough, "Before I was reduced to being only half a man? I have admittedly recently been made bitterly aware of my handicap, but I believe I can still manage to take care of myself."

"I'm sorry. I shouldn't have said that. But you still insist on treating this as some kind of game. I assure you some of these men are in deadly earnest."

"Including Baggett?" he inquired steadily.

She looked up quickly and then seemed to be unable to tear her eyes away. With her eyes locked on his, he suddenly felt as if his heart might burst through his tight waistcoat, and discovered he was breathing as if he had run a mile. But he recognized that she was dangerously on edge, and tried to ease some of the tension between them.

"At any rate, I beg you not to spoil it. I think the thing that first attracted me about you was the fact that you were so obviously wholly indifferent to my handicap. Most of the women I meet seem to take instant pity on me and want to soothe my aching brow with their soft hands. Unfortunately, I could never abide being made an object of compassion."

She gave a low laugh and abruptly stripped off her gloves and held her hands out to him. "Then you needn't worry! I have no soft white hands to soothe your aching brow, nor is compassion—or any other of the feminine virtues, for that matter—one of my strong suits. If the truth be known, I'm far more accustomed to mucking out stables than pouring tea in a lady's drawing room. Haven't you discovered that yet?"

He captured her hands and held them steadily against her sudden convulsive attempt to free them. When he turned them over, she tried to close her fingers over her callused palms, but he gently prevented her. "No—don't be ashamed of such hands, sweetheart," he said quietly. "Why do you think I fell in love with you almost at first sight, except that you were wholly unlike all the spoiled, useless women I've known all my life?"

"Because of my ruined hands?" She tried to make a joke of it, then abruptly stilled as his words seemed to penetrate. her eyes again rose to meet his, her face suddenly deathly pale. "*What* did you say?" she whispered, beginning to tremble as if she had a fever.

He began to look amused. "Why else did you think I'd proposed to you if I hadn't fallen in love with you, you little fool?"

"How should I know? Insanity, most like!" she retorted, trying to recover her slip.

"That kind of insanity doesn't happen to run in my family. You can't really imagine I go around proposing marriage to every woman I meet on a whim? How on earth did you imagine I'd remained a bachelor all these years, if so?"

"I don't know—I didn't think. But you'll admit that sanity doesn't figure strongly in anything you've done to date," she cried distractedly. "Deciding to race a horse on a whim, proposing marriage to the tomboyish granddaughter of an admitted Irish rogue. You're obviously either insane or still suffering from delayed fever!"

He smiled down at her with great tenderness. "Neither, I assure you. But if you're looking for an explanation, I can't give it to you. All I know is that I took one look at you and knew instantly that you were the only woman in the world for me. Believe me, I felt almost as stunned as you look, for I'd begun to doubt it would ever happen to me. But it has, and I've decided not to fight it."

Again she made a convulsive attempt to pull her hands away. "My God! You are mad," she breathed. "You clearly should be locked up in Bedlam."

He laughed, and raised her hands to his lips and pressed a kiss into each work-roughened palm.

She jerked as if she had been burned, and tried desperately to pull them away, but he held them strongly, refusing to release her.

"You may turn that sharp tongue of yours on everyone else," he said a little unsteadily, "but I warn you now: I won't permit you to insult the woman I love."

"And I don't know why I waste my time trying to convince you," she cried. "Even when I tell you the truth, you willfully refuse to believe me. You obviously deserve everything that's coming to you."

"You warned me about your companions, and I confess I take exception to one of them at least," he said lightly.

He recognized the dangerous volatility of her mood, if he did not completely understand the reason for it, and was treading lightly. "In fact, if I ever see him pawing you again, I warn *you* I shall do my best to knock his teeth down his oily throat."

She looked startled, then flushed a little. "Baggett?" she said contemptuously. "He needn't worry you."

"So your grandfather says. But then, it's not myself I'm worried about."

She looked up quickly. "You discussed Baggett with Sir James? I can guess how far that got you. At any rate, I can take care of Baggett. But if you object to him, you should be warned, for I believe he's one of the more respectable of my acquaintances."

"Why does your grandfather dislike him so?"

She shrugged. "Sir James dislikes anyone who is more successful a rogue than he is."

"I think you underestimate your grandfather, my sweet. He is admittedly highly colorful and annoying, but he seems harmless enough."

Her laugh sounded almost hysterical. "No, it's you who underestimates him. I learned long ago not to. I even love him, God help me, but I sometimes think he's capable of anything. And thanks to his tutelage, so am I! *So am I!* So be warned. Get away before it's too late."

For answer he gathered her hands closer to his chest, holding them tightly. "Sweetheart, can't you trust me?" he asked gently. "It's been evident to me almost since I came that you're in some sort of trouble. Can't you realize yet that I'm unlikely to be shocked by anything, and I want only to help?"

"Damn you," she cried in a sudden passion. "Oh, God, why did you have to be so *nice*?"

His heart stirred painfully, but he couldn't help laughing

as well. "Good God. Is that what you think me? *Nice?* God help me, you could hardly have damned me with fainter praise. If so, it's no wonder you won't marry me."

"But then, you don't know how rare that is in my world," she said bitterly. "Whatever else I am, I'm not *nice*. But it seems I still possess some inconvenient vestiges of conscience. I beg you, if you really c-care for me, against all rhyme or reason, then go away and leave me alone! That's the only way you can help me. Just leave me alone."

He was frowning, and would have pressed her, but just at that moment a familiar drawling voice said in amusement from behind them, "So here you are. Hardly the locale I would have chosen for a *tête-à-tête*—but then, each to his own taste. The groom out there said I might find you here."

Cat jumped as if she'd been shot, and convulsively pulled her hands away, and Simon could have cursed his friend's inconvenient timing. But he made the necessary introductions.

Cat was far from being at her best, for she looked sullen, and answered any remark addressed directly to her in monosyllables. Simon knew that look very well, and again could have cursed Jack for forcing her back into her protective shell.

Fortunately Jack was prefectly capable of single-handedly keeping a light flow of inconsequential chatter going, for he received little help from either of them. If he sensed that he had interrupted an awkward scene, he did not reveal it.

Nor was the effort required of him for long. Cat soon found an excuse to hurry away. As they strolled back to the curricle, Major Robinette remarked casually, casting a shrewd glance at his old friend, "Well, at least I'm beginning to understand. She's very beautiful."

Simon started, as if he had forgotten his presence. "Which reminds me: what the devil are you doing here?"

"Oh, just having a look around the area. And it wasn't hard to guess where you'd be."

"Just sticking your long nose into my affairs, you mean!" Then he drew a deep breath. "Oh, the devil! I'm sorry, Jack. I don't mean to take my ill temper out on you. But I'm beginning to fear things must be even worse than I thought."

His friend glanced at him again, and hesitated, as if uncertain whether to say something or not. At last he said, as if unwillingly, "While I was waiting for you this morning, I overheard some interesting local gossip. If you really want to know what your Miss Dunraven is hiding, I think I may be able to tell you."

When Simon looked incredulously at him, he added grimly. "According to the rumors, she means to enter a horse named Dunraven's Folly against yours in the Two Thousand Guineas race."

15

"Cat, he told Sir James he means to marry you."

Cat had resumed her interrupted work, and at her brother's incredulous words did not bother to look up. In fact she was grateful her back was to Jamie so he could not see the betraying color that invaded her face. "A temporary madness, no doubt," she answered flippantly. "He'll soon get over it."

She could feel Jamie staring at her, trying to read through her defenses, but she deliberately kept her back to him.

"Don't you care?" he asked quietly at last. "I must confess that when he told me, my first thought was a surge of relief and happiness. If you ask me, he's just the man for you. Except that—"

Cat did look round then, bitter mockery on her face. "Exactly. I wondered when that was going to occur to you. Except that I've lied and cheated from the beginning and have every hope my horse will beat his in the Two Thousand," she finished for him. "But then, we can always hope he's so besotted by my fatal beauty that he'll even manage to overlook that, along with my birth and rather unfortunate reputation. Only somehow I suspect even he's not inclined to be that mad."

Jamie was looking troubled. "Don't, Cat! I hate it when you belittle yourself that way. If you ask me, he'd be damned lucky to win you. At any rate, surely you can't still mean to go through with it? I mean . . . I don't want to sound grasping, but Lord Simon must be at least as wealthy as Baggett. Surely there's no longer any need . . ."

She managed an unamused smile. "There's every need. Even if he shouldn't come to his senses and realize just how . . . ridiculous a marriage between us would be—and you may be sure his friends and family will take good care to point out all the difficulties to him, if they haven't occurred to him already. But how is he going to feel when he discovers what's going on? Or haven't you thought of that either?"

Jamie plainly considered it now, and didn't like the answer he reached. "Damn Sir James," he swore. "This is all his doing. I only wish he could realize how his scheme has backfired this time."

"Aye, he's the one who set our feet to the maze we're now treading, as always," she acknowledged. "But it was doomed from the beginning. Sir James admittedly brought him here by trickery, and means to use him for his own purposes. But I've had to face that I'm little better. God help me, I even told him he might take Lord Simon for as much as he liked, so long as he didn't spoil my game."

She brushed the escaping hair from her flushed face and laughed a little harshly. "I didn't know then, of course, just how high the stakes were likely to be. But it makes little difference. I deserve everything that's coming to me."

"But damnit, you didn't know Sir James meant to enter his horse in the Two Thousand against Folly. At any rate, you haven't done anything wrong! You know as well as I do that you've given his horse better training than he'd get anywhere else."

"But is anyone else likely to believe that?" she demanded

cynically. "Unless Conqueror were to win, and he's not going to do that. Believe me, I've been over and over it until my head reels, and there's no way out of the maze. Even if I were to scratch Folly now, it's far too late. Lord Simon's unlikely to believe I didn't know what was going on from the beginning."

"Yes, but—"

"There are no buts. Nor do I dare scratch Folly. I lack Sir James's reckless instincts, I fear. To risk everything on the unlikely chance that Lord Simon will in the end be able to overlook both my birth and my deceit carries far too unattractive odds for me. No man can be that magnanimous."

Then she shrugged. "At any rate, the truth is, I've no yen to play such a role, even if he could. If I were to marry him in the face of all there is between us, how long do you think it would be before he came to hate me—or I him, for that matter? I fear I'm temperamentally unsuited to play for long the shrinking wife, obliged to be grateful for every crumb from her lord's table and never able to forget his condescension in marrying her."

"But that's ridiculous! If he really loves you, he would never—"

"No, perhaps not," she admitted wearily. "But I would. It seems I am enough Sir James's granddaughter to prefer my pride, even to so advantageous a marriage."

Then she lifted her shoulders, as if shaking off a burden. "And he . . . he will soon enough be relieved at his escape. It seems there is too much between us for either of us to ever completely forget."

It was obvious that Jamie was struggling against the unpleasant truth of her words. "Do you love him?" he asked in a low voice at last.

She hesitated. "Too well to risk seeing him come to despise me. But don't worry. I have little enough faith in love, I fear.

I am not going to pine away for lack of it. I learned that lesson too well from our mother.''

"But at least you can't mean to marry Baggett now?" insisted Jamie.

She made herself smile. "Let's hope there will be no need. If Folly wins, we will be able to redeem the note on the Downs and even buy you a pair of colors. And don't insist again that you won't leave me, for if you think it makes me happy to see you mooning around here, worried the war will end without you, you're sadly mistaken. If that happens, I will marry Baggett, and you'll have no excuse left for remaining.''

Jamie still looked unconvinced, so she added for good measure, "At any rate, it's all for the best. I'll admit I was briefly tempted by the thought of becoming 'my lady,' but racing's in my blood, you know that. I would be like a fish out of water away from it. And how long do you think Lord Simon would be content with a wife who insisted upon mucking out her own stables, and hobnobbing with his grooms and ostlers instead of paying social calls on the local gentry? The truth is, Sir James has done us both a favor. Now, go away and let me finish, or we'll be until midnight settling the horses in for the night.''

But long after Jamie had gone, still looking troubled, she leaned against one of the stable walls and made no attempt to return to her task. Her fist was against her mouth, and she was staring dry-eyed at the endless progression of dreary and hopeless days before her, and wondering at the capacity of human nature to intentionally destroy itself.

And she was to have to begin facing them even sooner than she had dreaded, for when she came down to dinner the next evening, it was to find that Sir James had met Lord Simon in town and invited him to come back and take potluck with them.

She checked at the doorway, suddenly bitterly aware of her shabby gown, the even shabbier room, and the probable inferior nature of the dinner shortly to be set before them. But it was too late to draw back, and so she had no choice but to enter the room and greet their guest.

The men rose politely, Jamie looking at her with some anxiety. But she saw no one else, for since she had last seen him, Lord Simon had changed in some ineffable way. He greeted her politely enough, but there was a new, hard look in the back of his eyes, and the familiar lurking amusement was completely gone.

So. He knew, then. For a moment her heart nearly betrayed her, and she knew a curious empty feeling, as if she had lost something infinitely precious. Then her chin rose, for she had always known this minute must come. She had never been one to put off the painful or unpleasant in the hopes that it would miraculously go away. In her experience it never did, and the delay only made the inevitable that much more painful in the end.

But the evening seemed to be interminable. Dinner was every bit as bad as she had feared, and the evening was saved from being a total disaster only by Sir James's usual refusal to recognize the awkwardness of the situation and Lord Simon's exceedingly good manners.

Jamie, too, seemed oddly silent, but Sir James was in a high good humor and for some reason seemed insistent upon drawing out his noble guest.

Lord Simon answered his queries politely enough, but his usual charm was noticeably absent, and his reminisces of camp life tended toward general mishaps associated with campaign living and incidents in which he himself appeared in a far-from-heroic light.

At Sir James's prompting he reluctantly told of one occasion when he and a fellow officer were returning late from visiting friends in a nearby regiment, and had gotten lost in the dark, only to eventually find themselves behind the French lines.

"Their captain was very gracious, however, and even gave us supper before setting us straight and giving us a safe-conduct through the lines. But we were sweating at first, I can tell you. We could envision the ignominy of becoming French prisoners without a single shot being fired. And we didn't soon hear the last of it either, I fear. For months after, our friends roasted us about it."

Sir James, rapidly mellowing under the influence of the heavy burgundy served with dinner, chuckled appreciatively. "Aye, I've always said war is the only place, barring the turf, of course, where a man can experience real adventure. If there'd been a war going on when I was a lad—and I except that foolish fiasco in the colonies, of course, for I'm too Irish to fight to deprive anyone else of his liberties—who knows? My life might have turned out very differently. I well remember the time . . ."

He then launched into a highly amusing anecdote of his own, his accent, as it always did when he was drinking, becoming even more pronounced than usual.

"Aye, those were the days," he concluded nostalgically, draining his glass once more. "Here, lad, your glass is empty. Caity, me girl, it's a bad hostess ye are to let such a thing happen! But enough of that fancy French eye-water! Poteen's what we need, for there's a drink worthy of a man."

Cat shrugged and rose silently to produce a bottle of whiskey. She had said very little throughout the protracted meal, and though she had from time to time caught Lord Simon's steady eyes on her, they had said almost nothing to one another.

That would no doubt come later—if he could still walk, that is. Sir James had no doubt invited him there for some purpose of his own, and seemed intent on making his guest drink himself into fuzzy-headedness at the very least. More than once he had insisted upon filling Lord Simon's glass, despite his protestations that he had no head for wine since his illness; and the production of the heavy Irish whiskey would undoubtedly soon have him under the table if he were foolish enough to drink it. She shrugged again, telling herself she was not his keeper.

And certainly Lord Simon made no objection when Sir James, as usual, unaware of or indifferent to any undercurrents in the room, poured the three men a generous measure. "It's not the same now, of course," he added almost wistfully. "In the old days a man could win a fortune or lose it in one day, and there was excitement enough and challenge to appeal to any man. Now the sport's become so hedged round with rules and long-nosed moralizers, I scarce recognize it any longer. Ah, bah! Bad cess to 'em, I say." He emptied his glass and reached to refill it, lifting it in a silent toast to his guest.

Cat had stiffened, for that was a dangerous topic, but Lord Simon dutifully lifted his own glass and swallowed most of its contents. Then he glanced at Cat and remarked, as if deliberately, "I fear I must disagree with you, sir. In fact I would hardly say the sport is hedged round with too many rules."

Cat felt herself paling, but Sir James complained, "Ah, nonsense! Ye've been listening too much to Caity, I fear. She's grown to be so cautious I scarcely recognize her of late."

Lord Simon's eyes were again on Cat, though this time she refused to raise her own to meet them. "You surprise me, sir. In fact, 'cautious' is the last word I would use to describe Miss Dunraven,'' he responded rather grimly.

Cat desperately wanted to escape, but would not give him the satisfaction of seeing her flee. "Come, now! You, if anyone, should know that ye won't rid the turf of the riffraff and hangers-on, lad, any more than ye will an army,'' insisted Sir James. "Rules and all this moralizin' only make things worse.''

"Very well. There's a certain amount of truth in that, sir.'' The major's eyes had, thankfully, returned to his host. "But while there is unfortunately an occasional need for war, I believe any man who claims truthfully to like it is not to be trusted. And while God knows excesses do happen, most of us try very hard not to allow the more brutal elements inevitably attracted to the army to ever gain the ascendance. When that happens, you no longer have an army, but a mindless mob. I've seen it a few times and I hope never to see it again.''

"Ah, now you sound like your father and the other respectable members of the Turf Club. They think to clean up the sport without diminishin' any of its excitement, and I tell ye the thing's impossible. And if they ever succeed, God help me, that's the day I give it up forever and sit back waitin' to die. And ye certainly won't rid the turf of such things by makin' speeches in Parliament and formin' gentlemen's associations to police the sport. Police the sport! Ye might as well try to make an Irishman give up poteen, or love an Orangeman for that matter, as hedge a true sportsman round with rules and societies.''

Abruptly Cat rose, unable to remain and listen to it any longer. "If you'll excuse me,'' she said in a strangled voice, "I . . . need some fresh air.'' She almost fled from the room.

It was several hours later before she at last heard the

breakup of the party. She wondered cynically if Lord Simon was capable of making it home all right or if he would have to be helped to bed by his valet. But then she deliberately hardened her heart against the thought. Certainly if he had been drinking poteen all this time under Sir James's tutelage, he was likely to be blind drunk by now.

When the door opened quietly behind her, she spoke without turning around. "How much did Sir James manage to take the major for, Jamie?"

"I'm sorry to disappoint you," answered the calm voice that had been disturbing her dreams for far too long now. "But I learned a long time ago not to play cards with as downy an old bird as your grandfather."

Then his voice hardened slightly. "Besides, I've learned recently I have little taste for . . . sport, I'm afraid."

Cat stiffened, for she had thought she would have at least until tomorrow before she must confront him. She closed her eyes briefly, then at last turned slowly to face him and said deliberately, "Very wise. But I fear it's a trifle too late for that, don't you think?"

He ignored that, and limped on into the room. He looked perfectly sober, and apart from a certain tiredness, as if he had sat too long on his injured leg, seemed remarkably fresh. It was impossible to read his mood, which she was beginning to realize was one of his chief faults.

As if to bear out her words, he grimaced. "At any rate, I'm afraid I'm not yet up to the prolonged after-dinner sessions over the port—or poteen—that are expected of a gentleman. I've never cared for getting foxed, and I couldn't sit for many hours without getting up and moving around, even before my injury."

"What happened to Jamie and my grandfather?" she demanded abruptly.

He looked momentarily amused. "Your brother is putting

Sir James to bed. It seems he hasn't the head for poteen that he used to.''

She knew she was staring at him incredulously. "Sir James hasn't the head . . . ?" Either yours must be made of iron, or you managed somehow to escape drinking poteen with him. It's usually lethal to anyone not used to it.''

He gratefully went to stand before the small fire, and turned his back to it, leaning his shoulder on the mantel. "Oh, I've a surprisingly hard head," he said mildly. "You had to have, in my regiment.''

He nodded to the bottle and glass before her and added politely, "Is that why you're sticking to brandy, by the way?''

She flushed, then lifted her glass defiantly. "I've decided to discover for myself the healing properties of alcohol. And oddly enough, for once Sir James may actually have been right. Why, are you shocked to find your hostess tossing back brandy instead of daintily sipping tea in the drawing room? Doesn't it happen in the best London households?''

She drained her glass, but spoiled the effect somewhat by gasping as the harsh spirit caught the back of her throat.

He regarded her steadily. "I have learned to be shocked by nothing you do, Miss Dunraven. But you should never drink alone. Mind if I join you?''

16

Cat laughed harshly and filled her glass again. This time it went down more easily, without seeming to burn the whole way. "Help yourself. Only let's stop fencing, for God's sake! You know, don't you?"

He eyed her steadily, and she was surprised that she had ever thought him weak. He was so innately civilized and decent that it seemed he would never bluster or swear as Sir James would have done. But she was beginning to discover that quiet anger could sometimes be far more formidable than an outright explosion. For the first time it occurred to her that she had reason to be afraid of him.

"Yes, I know," he said quietly at last. "I have only one question. Did you ever intend to tell me yourself or did you mean to let me wait until the day of the race to find out."

She wanted to weep, but instead made her voice sound deliberately hard and indifferent. "Why should you be surprised? You've known what I am from the beginning."

He laughed then, and it was somehow more painful to her than any amount of cursing would have been. "Well, at least you're honest," he admitted. "I refused to believe it at first when Jack told me. Of course I was reluctantly forced to believe it, for the evidence has been right before my eyes from the beginning, hasn't it? I even saw you on the black myself, God help me, and had the temerity to warn you against him. But I must confess I still don't begin to understand why. In God's name, *why*? Is it the excitement? Does racing really mean that much to you?''

"Yes! Damn you, yes!'' she cried, wanting only to have it over with. "I'm my grandfather's granddaughter, after all. You knew that too from the beginning.''

"So it would seem. You could have had anything I possessed, but I suppose I was foolish to imagine even an offer of marriage could compete against that. Especially to one in my . . . useless condition.''

She wanted to protest, but knew it was safest to let him think even that, if it would send him away sooner. She also numbly noticed the use of the past tense, and could only be grateful that the brandy must be finally beginning to take effect.

"Anything you possess?'' she repeated almost wearily. "Did it never occur to you that your honorable proposal of marriage strips me of more pride than Baggett's insults? At least I have something to offer him in return. But I have nothing to offer you. Except, of course, the magnanimity you must feel at being able to overlook all my drawbacks. And if that is all there is between us, how long before you begin to despise me?''

A little muscle was jumping in his jaw. "I . . . see. I had no idea my offer of marriage was nothing more than an insult. In fact, I had flattered myself you were . . . beginning to care for me just a little. It seems I am as capable of willful deception as your grandfather.''

"God knows we are all capable of that.''

His mouth twisted a little bitterly. "Yes. There seems nothing more to be said, then.''

It was odd how so few words could spell the death knell to all her dreams. "No. I'll have the bay ready to leave tomorrow."

But he lifted his head at that, as if it were the last thing he had expected her to say. "The bay? What the devil has this got to do with the bay?"

She stared at him, thinking the brandy must have betrayed her after all, for she could not have understood him. "What has . . . ? Everything, obviously. You can't wish to leave him here now."

"Why not? You needn't fear I would . . . force myself on you any longer, and it seems a little late to change trainers. The race is only a week away, after all."

"Late to change trainers?" She shook her head as if to clear it, then was sorry, as it set the room spinning around her. "Have you run mad or have I? What have we just been talking about if not trainers?"

But abruptly he had taken the brandy glass from her lax fingers and had set it on the table beside her. "I think you've had enough of this," he said surprisingly. "I fear you'll suffer already in the morning."

"What does it matter?" she demanded bitterly. "At any rate, I've mixed enough dampers in my life to know what to do for it."

Incredibly, there was a hint of laughter in his voice now. "I knew from the beginning you would make an excellent wife, but I never before suspected just how good. But for now I want you to tell me in plain and simple English what the devil you think we're talking about."

Cat gratefully allowed her eyes to drift closed for an instant. It seemed he wanted his pound of flesh, and meant her to admit everything to him. If so, he could have it. "Very well. Between us, my grandfather and I betrayed you from the beginning. He brought you here only to use your famous name, and I agreed to train your horse, knowing I was going to run my own in competition against you. Any trainer will tell you it would be the easiest thing in the world for me to make sure Conqueror doesn't win on the day of the race. I have only to slack off on his training, or run him too long the day before the race, or give him the wrong feed, and you'd never be able to prove a thing. Does that satisfy you? Is that what you wanted to hear?''

Abruptly he was sitting beside her, and had pulled her heavy head onto his warm shoulder. When she tried to resist, he held her tightly in the crook of his arm and said rather unsteadily, "No, lie still. I warned you you might not like the effects of brandy after all. In fact, I should undoubtedly send you up to bed, but it seems I am . . . not quite the gentleman I had always thought myself, and this conversation is suddenly becoming of immense interest to me. And I fear I am very far from being satisfied. If you were plotting against me, as you say, then why did you try so hard to send me away?''

She laughed bitterly. "What difference does it make? You refused to go.''

Again he sounded amused. "Yes, I refused to go. And do you know why? Because I fell in love with you the moment I saw you. You little fool, did you really think I came today to accuse you of putting your own horse's chances above my own?''

She raised her head at that, thinking he must still be playing some kind of unkind game of cat and mouse with her. "What else? I . . . don't even blame you. But for what little it's worth, the bay never stood much chance of winning anyway. And I would never have allowed him to be hurt in any way.''

"I know that, my sweet," he said with an odd gentleness.

"But I fear I don't really give a damn about my horse's chances."

"You don't . . . I don't understand." But she had begun to tremble for some reason.

"That's more than obvious, my love. I may have had some notion I'd like to race horses, but the truth is, I discovered soon after coming here that there were too many things about the sport I disliked. I only stayed to have a continued excuse to see you. I thought it must be painfully obvious to everyone. Certainly Chicklade knew—and probably your canny grandfather as well. If Conqueror never ran a single race, I wouldn't care."

She had to close her eyes again weakly. "Then why were you so angry?" she whispered.

Abruptly his face hardened again. "Because whatever your pride, my stubborn little love, I won't have you risking your neck for two thousand guineas. Good God, did you really think I'd stand tamely by and let you do such a thing?"

"Risking my . . . I think I must have had too much brandy to drink. None of this makes any sense any longer," she complained, letting her head fall back weakly onto his shoulder.

"Then I'll make it even simpler. I don't give a damn if your horse runs against mine, and I never for one moment suspected you of risking the bay's chances. But I tell you right now I won't have you riding that devil-spawned black of yours in the race. Is that clear enough for you?"

"You thought . . . you thought *I* meant to ride Folly?" she demanded.

"Of course I did. Who else? I know enough of that black devil of yours by now to know that no one else can handle him, you little witch."

"But I'm not . . ." It was growing increasingly hard to

make her mind cooperate, but it was suddenly of immense importance that she make him understand. "Jem Chicklade is to ride him."

He was abruptly gripping her hands very tightly, and she could feel the urgent beat of his heart beneath her ear. "Is this true?" he demanded.

Then his voice changed ludicrously. "Sweetheart! Don't cry, my love. It's all right."

"Oh, God," she wept, beating ineffectually against his broad chest. "Why did you have to come to spoil everything? I was happy enough before you came. It was cruel of you—*cruel*—to leave me with no defenses left against you, not even my pride."

He was half-laughing, half-groaning, as he easily stilled her weak outburst and pressed a kiss on her soft curls. "And I think you are dangerously vulnerable right now—and I am too tempted to take unfair advantage of the fact. Certainly for a sensible woman you're uttering a good deal of nonsense. The last thing I mean is to be cruel to you, and I want no defenses left between us, don't you know that yet? If the race really means so much to you, I won't interfere. I don't approve, for I think Folly dangerously unstable, but so long as you don't mean to ride him yourself—which I admit now was indeed a fantastic notion—then I'll say no more. But what happens then? Have you thought that far?"

She shrugged, but the gesture was weakened by the fact that she had no will left to pull herself away from his comfortable embrace. "If Folly wins, then we continue as we are for a little longer. Or at least until my grandfather finally loses everything on a sure wager he couldn't refuse. And if Folly loses, then the end merely comes a bit sooner. I'm not so big a fool as to think it will really change anything. But I have to try—don't you see that?"

"I see only that you are the woman I never thought to find," he answered thickly. "And that I adore you. I also see that you are delightfully tipsy at the moment, and thus perhaps not in the best state to grasp what I'm going to say. But I will tell you anyway. Do you know what's going to happen regardless of whether Folly wins or loses? You are going to wed me. I will reluctantly give you until then, because I can see it's important to you. But then I mean to claim you, if I have to carry you forcibly to Gretna Green to do it. And there will be no more talk of pride between us. Do I make myself very clear?"

She opened her eyes to find his face surprisingly close to her own, so that she could see the attractive laugh lines at the corners of his eyes, and the becoming color he was beginning to recapture after his long illness. She knew she should be trying to talk some sense into him—make him understand the bitterness and regret that could follow in an unequal marriage, after the first fine rapture had worn off.

But it was somehow hard to form the words, and her mind kept insisting upon slippng away to inconsequential matters instead. She could see the still-faint lines of pain between his fair brows, and suddenly wanted to reach up and smooth them away, as if the very act could cure his suffering.

"My poor sweet," he said, his voice sounding very far away. "Have you heard anything I've said? No matter. I'll remind you again in the morning. For the moment, this will suffice."

And then he was kissing her. She should have protested or turned her head away, but she suddenly found she was too breathless to gather her scattered wits. She had been kissed a few times before—distasteful stolen fumblings from drunken or overconfident fools, mistaking her position for an open invitation. She had always emerged feeling besmirched, and had never seen why kissing could be considered a pleasurable activity.

But now she began to understand all too well, for Simon's lips did strange things to her equilibrium. They were neither hurtful nor distasteful, but warm and gentle, as if against all odds he instinctively knew how inexperienced she was.

All she knew was that she had never before experienced such a rush of blood pounding in her veins, or such excitement outside of a hard-won race. She tried to tell herself it was the brandy, but she knew instinctively that the alcohol had had nothing to do with it.

He was finally the one to pull away, for she was as spineless as a jellyfish, and would have been content to lay bemusedly in his arms forever. "I never understood it before," she said wonderingly when she could manage to speak again. "But I finally begin to see why my mother could have given up everything for the sake of love."

He laughed unsteadily, sounding well-pleased with himself, and smoothed the halo of dark hair away from her face with a tenderness she had only known, long ago, from one other person.

"And I am beginning to understand that I can't live without you much longer," he said. "But I fear it's more than time I was going. When you come to me—and that will be very soon now, my darling!—I want it to be voluntarily and with every faculty alert, not half-tipsy and three-quarters asleep and wholly adorable. And that, my stubborn little love, is a promise."

She tried again to protest, but her lashes were suddenly too heavy to lift. "A promise you can't keep," she mumbled sleepily.

"Oh, yes, I can, sweetheart." He sounded supremely confident. "I confess there have been times before when I've doubted it, but not anymore."

She should have disabused his mind of that curious over-confidence. She had long ago accepted that there could be no future between them. But she was too tired to make the effort. The last thing she remembered was the light feel of his lips against her eyes and cheeks and mouth, as insubstantial as a butterfly's wings. Then she was asleep, feeling safer and more content than she had ever felt in her life before.

17

When Simon saw Cat the next morning, she looked pale and in an ill humor. She was talking to Joe Chicklade when he drove up, but at sight of him she promptly turned and strode away.

It was Chicklade himself who went to the horses' heads, a heretofore unlooked-for honor.

He greeted the major pleasantly enough, then added with what in another man might almost have been dry humor, "Happen Miss Cat is not her best this morning, sir."

The major looked at him sharply but was careful to keep any betraying knowledge from his own face. "No? Nothing serious, I hope?"

"No. But if you was to be looking for her, I don't doubt you'd find her in the south paddock," he further volunteered.

The major thanked him thoughtfully. So far Simon had been singularly unsuccessful either in winning the groom's confidence or in understanding what role he played. He seemed to be devoted to his employers, and according to Aikins was competent and well-thought-of in the neighborhood. But he seemed to go about his duties in a quiet, unassuming way and kept largely to himself.

Aikins had once seen him in one of the taprooms in

Newmarket and tried deliberately to draw him out. But though Chicklade had accepted a pint of bitter, and been pleasant enough, he had been closemouthed to the point of reticence and did not linger long.

But Chicklade hesitated now, then surprised the major still more by adding, "If you don't mind my asking, Major, what's your interest in Miss Cat? I know it's not my place to ask, but I've been lookin' after her since she was a tiny girl, seems like, and I just wondered."

The major grinned at him. "I have not the least objection to your asking. In fact, it's no secret. I have every intention of making Miss Cat my wife—if I have to kidnap her to do it."

Chicklade shifted the straw in his mouth, but his expression seemed to have softened slightly. "Then happen you've got your work cut out for you," he said wryly. "Miss Cat's never yet accepted a hand on her bridle, and likely never will."

"I have no intention of trying to break her spirit. But I do have every intention of helping her."

"Then good luck to you. But I should perhaps warn you: Miss Cat don't take to trust easily."

The major sobered. "I know, and that's something I hope to change, Chicklade. But in the meantime, if she should ever need me—for any reason—you know where to find me."

Chicklade nodded and led the chestnuts away, seeming well-satisfied.

Simon found Cat in the south paddock, as Chicklade had predicted, taking Conqueror through his paces. As he limped over the rough ground toward her, the major watched her in reluctant admiration. He had learned over the past weeks that here was no task connected with the stables that was beneath her or that she was incapable of doing, no matter how dangerous or dirty. Just as he had caught her mucking out the stables on that one memorable occasion, he had seen her risk her neck time and again under flying hooves. She also undertook tirelessly the grueling and repetitive work that seemed to be a large part of horse training. He wanted to take her away from all of it. But if she insisted, he was prepared to buy an estate near Newmarket for her and fulfill his original intention of setting up a stud.

She glanced around as he limped up, but finished with what she was doing before at last walking over. It was obvious that her softened mood from the night before had completely vanished. "Well?" she demanded belligerently. "Have you come to gloat?"

"Gloat over what? Your inevitable headache? I've had one too often myself to feel superior, believe me."

"I am perfectly well aware I made a fool of myself last night!"

His face softened and he smiled down at her. "On the contrary. You did fall asleep on my shoulder after a long and tiring day, and I won't deny that I thoroughly enjoyed the experience. But in case you're worried, I left you sleeping peacefully and called to your brother to carry you upstairs to bed. It's not that I wouldn't have liked the honor, but I am hardly up to the demands of the stairs yet."

He saw the relief in her eyes, and added ruefully, "Yes, I suspected you had some such suspicion in your mind. I can only repeat: you did nothing last night either to shock or repel me. Again, quite the contrary."

"I have a vivid recollection of every foolish thing I said, so don't patronize me," she snapped.

"I hope you have a vivid recollection of everything *I* said as well, then, but we'll go into that later. Are you talking about your grandfather's reason for inviting me here? I did find that rather interesting, I confess, though I'm afraid I didn't wholly understand quite how my horse or my reputation can help your grandfather.''

"Then I'll explain it to you," she said contemptuously. "Baggett, who owns the favorite in the Two Thousand Guineas, has brought in a ringer. He means to—''

"Wait a minute. A ringer? That's a four-year-old meant to run as a three-year-old, isn't it?"

"Yes. Baggett is hoping to thoroughly confuse the betting ring. At the moment, no one knows which of his horses carries his money, and he's taking care to keep it that way. It's not yet generally known that he owns both, but Sir James can always find out things before anyone else does. He thinks Baggett intends to pull his own favorite. And that's why he brought in your horse—to muddy the waters still further. Haven't you noticed that Conqueror is drawing surprising odds for a completely unknown colt?''

Simon was frowning by now. "I have, of course, but I must confess I didn't give it much thought. Let me be sure I've got this straight. Your friend Baggett means to run a four-year-old in a race of three-year-olds, against his own horse, which is heavily favored to win. If the four-year-old wins, he'll earn better odds than if the favorite does, obviously. In the meanwhile, suspecting that he means to pull a fast one, your grandfather imported my horse, and has convinced the ring its chances are better than they are, in order to further confuse the betting. Is that right?''

"Exactly."

When he burst out laughing, she added stiffly, "I'm glad you find it so amusing."

"Oh, I do! I do. In fact, it's almost priceless. My sweet nitwit, you're going to have to do better than that if you hope to discourage me. I told you I was looking for something to occupy my interest when I came. And believe me, I've found it.''

''You . . . you're not human,'' she whispered, as if against her will. ''No one could be as forgiving as you appear to be.''

''Oh, I'm very human—as you should know after last night. But about this ringer—surely something can be done? It is illegal, after all.''

She shrugged indifferently. ''Not without proof. And there won't be any proof. If it should happen to win, the losers may lodge a complaint, but until then the Jockey Club prefers to do nothing and hope the problem will never arise. Charming, isn't it?''

''Hmm,'' he said thoughtfully. ''I really begin to think that I shall have to take a hand in affairs, despite myself.'' He looked up and saw her watching him, and smiled at her with great affection. ''Never mind. And don't worry. I won't involve your grandfather, whatever happens. He's a wily old rogue, but I can't help liking him.''

Cat was almost to the point of believing that he really could do anything he set his mind to, but she merely said scathingly, ''Good God, do you think I fear that? Sir James has outwitted everyone for more than fifty years. He's invincible. But you still haven't grasped the truth yet, I fear. By talking up your horse, Sir James has almost guaranteed an attempt will be made to stop it. Especially since Baggett has it in for you anyway. And I warn you, he'll stop at nothing.''

''Then we'll just have to stop him, won't we?'' he inquired cheerfully. ''You don't know how glad I am to have something concrete to do at last. I was sick of sparring at shadows. And I always did enjoy a good fight—fair or no.''

''I'm beginning to think you *are* mad!''

"So you keep telling me. But if you do remember what I said last night, all that need concern you is that I meant every word of it. I have every intention of claiming you after the race—whatever happens. I'll be patient until then, but not a moment longer."

Cat stared after him as he limped away, for once in her life left with nothing to say.

In fact, she was finding it harder and harder to cling to her stubborn pride in the face of Lord Simon's surprisingly masterful demands. She had begun by thinking him charming but weak, but now she found she had developed a healthy respect for his will and courage, almost without her knowing how it had happened.

Even so, years of being able to depend on no one but herself prevented her from giving in to such weak impulses. She feared succumbing to the same unreality he obviously had, and she knew too well that nothing but heartbreak could result from that.

She could not deny that the major's absurd notion that she was somehow nobler than others of her sex was oddly flattering. But she had been humbled by too many years of slurs and slights, and the knowledge of her grandfather's reputation, to be able to believe it anything more than the idealistic delusions of a fever-starved brain.

At any rate, Major Lord Simon Grey, who could easily fit any woman's secret fantasy of the ideal lover, had no need to stoop so far beneath him in choosing a bride, and indeed every reason not to. He was at the moment still recovering from his wound, and obviously feeling himself, quite wrongly, something less than a man. But that would soon enough change.

He was also, she knew, struggling to come to terms with a very different life from the one he had planned for himself.

It was perhaps only natural that he should be temporarily inclined to mistake his feelings and emotions.

Aye, that was the way of it, however much she might wish it otherwise. And it would be both dishonorable and extremely foolish to take advantage of him at such a vulnerable time. She might gain a title and position through such a cheat, but unless she were completely without heart, she would soon enough come to rue her bargain. For the day would inevitably come when Lord Simon would waken to find himself shackled to a wife he was ashamed of, and could be forgiven for becoming bitter and angry.

Some women might think even that a worthwhile trade, but Cat was not among their number. She was herself too familiar, through her mother, with the bitter world of regret, and had no wish to subject either of them to it. Not for a hundred titles and estates would she barter her pride for the role of unwanted wife.

She'd even sooner marry Baggett, though that had long gone out of her plans. After Lord Simon it was somehow impossible to contemplate such an unspeakable match, even to save Sir James.

No, she knew her decision was the only one she could make. Hope to win the Two Thousand Guineas and redeem Sir James's note-of-hand and turn her back on any foolish dreams she might have had of a fairy-tale ending.

And even if it actually came to pass, against every likelihood: what then? as Lord Simon had asked. Marriage with him was clearly out of the question. The most she could hope for was to return to the same old life and the constant struggle to keep all their heads above water. And there was never any telling how long that would last before disaster struck again. Only until the next time Sir James got drunk and wagered more than he could afford to lose, or took some grand and highly improbable scheme in his head and mortgaged everything on a pipe dream.

No. If Lord Simon had done nothing else, he had made her finally take a long look at her life and come to despise herself as much as he would one day. She was through, whatever happened. If Folly won, then she could rescue her grandfather one last time, help Jamie achieve his dream, and walk away with a clear conscience.

Aye, that was the best plan. Disappear before she could be tempted to give in to Lord Simon's demands. She had no notion what she would do, for she had no money or prospects, and was woefully ill-equipped for any ladylike occupation. But one who was not fussy could undoubtedly find employment somewhere. She would even change her name if need be and invent a background as nondescript as her grandfather's had been colorful, for she had no scruples left. It was but another legacy from Sir James, and one that might be useful yet.

And if a rosy vision of what her life would be like as the major's adored and protected wife still insisted now and then upon intruding in this harsh reality, the more fool she. He had already given her more than he could know. For the first time in her life someone had seen her as desirable and worthy. It might be no more than the product of a fevered brain, and could not be expected to last, but she would always have the memory of it to cling to.

But even more important, he had shown her for the first time that a man could be kind and unselfish, and capable of generosity and trust. When he had been so angry yesterday, she had never doubted he had been protecting his own interests, and was merely furious at her for betraying him. It had not even occurred to her he might be worried for her own safety and didn't give a damn about his interests.

The truth had come as a blinding and liberating revelation to her. It had made her even more ashamed of her own actions, so that she could scarcely bear to meet his eyes. But it had also seemed to unlock some cold and long-forgotten place deep in her heart, where the ability to love and trust should have been.

Even more incredibly, he had obviously been frustrated, and disagreed with her, but he had had the decency and self-confidence not to try to stop her or to persuade her against her will to do what he wanted. He had respected her own needs and emotions, and threatened only to force her to marry him even against her will after the race was settled.

Well, that was safest not to think of, and doubtless when it came to the point, he wouldn't mean it. But he had shown her that not everyone lived in a world where mistrust was a way of life, where every word had to be questioned, and every act searched for a hidden motive. A world where lying and back-stabbing and villainy were everyday occurrences.

But still, she could not quite dismiss the half-dreaded hope that, against all rhyme or reason, the major was indeed serious, and mad enough to carry out his threat to marry her out of hand, if need be.

If so, what would her answer be? More than likely she would still be of the opinion that she must save him as well as herself from this quixotic madness. But if there was ever to be a chance for them, she knew instinctively that she must be able to come to him with her head held as high as possible, not out of weakness and need.

Well, *if* Folly won and they got out of debt, it would be time enough to think of that. She had long ago had to acknowledge to herself that she loved Major Lord Simon Grey almost to desperation.

Aye, that was the word for it, all right, she chided herself.

It was desperation even to think of it. And madness to think
that fairy tales might come true for such as her. It would
be enough to have Folly win, for that was fairy tale enough.
If she let herself dream of a masterful man come to sweep
her away from her unpleasant life, then she was a bigger
fool even than she had thought herself.

18

As the day of the race drew nearer, Cat's uncertainty and resultant tension only increased.

True to his word, Lord Simon had not pressed her, though in her present state of nerves Cat was no longer certain whether that was good or bad. Away from his presence it was fatally easy to believe he must indeed have come to his senses, as she had predicted, and already realized what a lucky escape he had had.

He did manage to make his presence felt, however, for somehow, without her quite knowing it, he had insinuated himself into the running of the Downs. For one thing, his groom, Aikins, had taken to hanging about and helping out at odd moments. When Cat had first come to hear of it, she was furious, and had had every intention of putting a stop to it at once. But as Chicklade pointed out, Aikins was both useful and unexpectedly tactful. He had asked to be allowed to help as a special favor, since he had little to do in Newmarket and was unused to being idle; and indeed, he seemed grateful for the occupation. He certainly was badly needed, since the injured groom was still laid up.

Cat knew perfectly well who was behind the offer, but for once finally managed to swallow her own pride. At any rate, she had nothing left to hide, and so gradually began to take Aikins' discreet presence for granted.

That he was there as much to ensure her safety as to relieve her of some of the more grueling work never occurred to her, and would undoubtedly have surprised and angered her. She had become so used to looking after herself that it came as second nature to her, and such male protectiveness was totally alien to her.

At any rate, she had enough to worry about already. Baggett had returned once or twice since that last unpleasant confrontation, but somehow or other either Chicklade or Aikins seemed to be hovering nearby or found an excuse to seek her out, so Baggett had been denied any opportunity to further his unwanted attentions or make himself any more unpleasant.

It did occur to her after the second time that the interruptions were far from coincidental. But since she had no desire for a *tête-à-tête* with Baggett, this time was only grateful for the interference.

At any rate, she knew Baggett was merely biding his time and that ultimately neither of her unlikely watchdogs could protect her from a confrontation. Only Baggett's supreme confidence in his ultimate victory undoubtedly persuaded him to such uncharacteristic patience now, for he was not a man to suffer frustration willingly.

But then, he could afford to wait. There was little doubt in anyone's mind that the Two Thousand Guineas race that year was going to be one of the dirtiest ever run in a very unclean sport. It was generally known by then that Baggett meant to enter both horses, and so rivalry was high to discover which of the two carried his own money. The colt Philanderer had long been his darling, and betting was high that Baggett would not pull his own favorite; but the more suspicious were convinced that the unknown Jerry had been rung in for that very reason.

Certainly it was widely rumored that Philanderer's own jockey was backing Jerry, and Baggett himself was said to have one hundred thousand guineas riding on the race.

As for the probable age of the newcomer, as Cat had suspected, no one was prepared to do anything about it until or unless Jerry actually won the race. And if, as seemed probable, Philanderer placed second, that would leave only one owner to protest the victory by an illegal horse, for only those actually placing in a race had the standing to protest any alleged illegalities.

Whatever the truth of the situation, Cat had her own, more immediate problems. As she had told Lord Simon, her grandfather's deliberate attempt to confuse the betting ring by bringing in the bay had only increased the likelihood of an attempt to nobble the horse. She had already dispatched Chicklade to sleep in the next stall, but she could not quiet her fears. She didn't think Lord Simon's bay had much chance of winning, but she was determined that nothing would keep him from a fair attempt.

The jockey she had chosen to ride him was an old friend, and reliable, but it was a sport in which no one could be completely trusted. She knew she was becoming obsessed with the problem, but could not seem to make herself stop worrying.

She was less worried about Folly. She knew he was probably the fastest horse in the ring, but though it was now widely known she meant to enter him, it was generally regarded as but another part of the same quixotry that had led her to buy him in the first place. No one seriously expected him to win, and he was still drawing extremely long odds. She only wished she could have afforded to back him heavily herself.

Jem Chicklade was sleeping in Folly's stall at night, but that was more a matter of taking every precaution than of any real fear for his safety. At any rate, Folly had too bad a reputation to make even the most unscrupulous of bettors willing to approach him, and she knew no one would get to him any other way. Young Jem was absolutely reliable, and she would have trusted his father with her own life.

Still, both tension and preparations intensified as the day approached. She was careful, the last few days before the race, not to overstress or tire either horse, and both were in the peak of condition. She was too experienced not to know that beyond that a good trainer could do no more. On the day of the race everything depended on the horse itself— and to a lesser extent its jockey. A bad jockey could make his move at the wrong time or deny a good horse a win, but no jockey could bring a bad or ill-prepared horse in to an undeserved victory.

The day before the race, Cat was oddly on edge. There was very little to do, and that day above all, she needed to keep busy. To cap it off, her grandfather was especially cheerful, which always worried her. She would have given much to know what he was up to, but knew from bitter experience not to ask him.

She did not see Lord Simon all day, and told herself she must be glad. Most owners haunted the stables the day before a race, increasing the horse's nervousness and badly irritating everyone else.

For her own part, she tried not to think of how much lay on the outcome of the race. But then, she was beginning to think his lordship had completely forgotten his unlikely ultimatum.

That thought was curiously unwelcome, whatever her answer must be. It seemed she was more feminine than she knew, for though she had no intention of taking him up on his capricious offer, it was less palatable that he should have forgotten the offer entirely. It seemed it would be as well when he was out of her life for good, for she was in danger of succumbing to such female weaknesses as she had always most despised.

But it did no good to think of any of that now. She ate very little dinner that night, though Sir James was in annoyingly high spirits himself, and excused herself to go to bed almost immediately thereafter.

She didn't expect to sleep, however, and wasn't disappointed. If any attempt was going to be made on Lord Simon's horse, it would be tonight or early tomorrow before the race. And the possibilities were almost unlimited. Horses had been poisoned, given bad feed, too much water, their jockeys bribed, their shoes tampered with, their saddles or bridles deliberately sabotaged or switched—almost anything could make the difference between victory and defeat for a highly nervous animal.

A trainer had to develop a certain fatalism, but for once Cat couldn't achieve her usual detachment. At last she rose and dressed and went back to the stables, unable to stay away any longer.

She found everything quiet. There was a full moon, so she hadn't bothered to bring a lantern. The stables seemed to be slumbering peacefully.

Too peacefully. She strolled across to Conqueror's stall, and he whickered to her gently and stuck his head over the half-door. But as she stroked his soft nose and crooned to him, there was no sign of Chicklade, who should have been in the next stall and whom she knew to be a very light sleeper.

Her heart began to beat faster, and she went to the next stall and called softly to him. But though she could see very little without a light, she received no answer and there was no sound of breathing or creaking of bedsprings when she went in.

He was not there. She tried to tell herself some emergency had called him away briefly, and she should be relieved, for she had half-feared finding him drugged or dead. But the hammering of her heart had increased to a violent tempo, and she regretted now the lack of a light. She suddenly felt vulnerable, and had to resist the temptation to look quickly behind her.

She went to the stall normally occupied by Folly, but this time no great black head came over the stall to greet her. The stall was completely empty, nor was there any sign of young Jem.

There had to be some explanation. A horse and two grown men could not simply disappear without a trace. She tried to think what to do, but found her mind was not functioning very well. The feeling that something was very wrong was growing in her, and she had to fight the urge to run back to the house and find Jamie or even Sir James.

She returned to Conqueror's stall, but there was still no sign of Chicklade or his son. She was about to give up and run back to the house to rouse it when some hint of sound froze her in her tracks.

The stableyard lay in full moonlight and so was well enough lit, though the edges and the stalls themselves lay in deep shadow. Her own dark habit lost itself in the blackness, but she was aware of a flicker of something across the yard, as of moonlight on a white shirt.

She resisted the impulse to call out sharply, and instead strained her eyes and ears in the darkness. Again there was a flicker of movement, but whoever it was was making an effort to walk stealthily, as if he had no desire to call attention to himself. It could not be Chicklade or Jem or one of the ostlers.

Then pandemonium seemed to erupt in the quiet yard. Even as she debated what to do, and wished she had thought to bring a pistol with her, she was grabbed from behind in hard arms, a rough hand clamping over her mouth, and lifted clear off her feet.

At the same moment, there was a flurry of movement across the yard. The figure she had seen, whether stalker or stalked, was tackled, and two heavy bodies went crashing and rolling painfully across the cobbled yard.

19

"Well, well!" growled a voice near Cat's ear. "It's the lady trainer. This is a stroke of luck. He'll pay even more for you, I reckon."

Cat tried to struggle, but she was being held too tightly to make much of an impact. She landed several not very effectual kicks, but her arms were caught in that iron grasp, and the hand over her mouth was making it difficult for her to catch her breath.

At the same time, the two bodies across the yard were locked in an equal, if more vocal, struggle. It was as if the familiar world of the stableyard had turned into a nightmare, for Cat recognized neither of the men's voices. She had no idea where Chicklade and his son could be, and was terrified for them, for it was obvious that an attempt had been made on the horses.

Then a familiar and wholly unexpected voice spoke from the intense darkness beside them. "Let her go. Now! Or the next breath you draw will be your last, I can promise you."

Cat had never heard that tone of voice from Simon before. He sounded calm and absolutely deadly, and her assailant was evidently taken by surprise as well, for he skewed her around toward the source of that voice. "What the . . . ?"

Cat could see now that Simon was standing there in the shadows holding a leveled pistol, which somehow seemed to add to the nightmare quality of the night. She had no idea what he was doing there or who else was with him, only that the fight across the yard seemed to have drawn reinforcements. Several voices had been added to the fray, but their own deadly little scene had not yet attracted any attention.

Then her captor obviously recognized the newcomer as well, for he laughed. "Well, if it ain't the crippled major," he sneered. "I heard you been sniffing around her skirts."

Cat saw the moonlight glint on Simon's whitened knuckles as his hand tightened, but he merely said, in that same hard voice, "You have five more seconds. One. Two. Three . . ."

Cat had ceased struggling, terrified of shifting the dangerous balance in any way. She knew as well as both of them must that her body provided an effective shield and that Simon would never dare to fire. And in any kind of fight, he would be hampered both by his own handicap and by the fear of hurting her.

Then she abruptly felt a minuscule bunching of muscles in the body bound so closely to hers, as the born horseman recognizes the slightest change in his mount's movements, and knew he meant to act. But the hand clamped so bruisingly over her mouth strangled her cry of warning in her throat, and she was helpless to prevent it.

"You want her, you got her!" The next moment she had been thrown bodily against Simon, and nothing she could do could save either of them.

She heard the man laugh again as Simon tried valiantly to withstand the impact. Only his supremely quick reflexes must have prevented her from being killed, for the pistol went off harmlessly to the side with a flash of light and a deafening roar, drawing a sudden startled silence from across the yard.

They both went down heavily, Simon on his bad leg, Cat an unwilling weight on top of him, half-stunned and deafened by the pistol shot. The breath was knocked from her and she was aware of a jolting pain in her left shoulder and arm as she struck the cobbles.

But she had no time for her own hurt. She scrambled off Simon, feeling the way he lay rigidly beneath her and half-terrified he had been shot himself. "Oh, God! Just lie still. I'll get help."

"That . . . won't be necessary," he said breathlessly. "I'm not . . . shot. Just my damned leg. Are you all right?"

"Yes. Even so, you shouldn't be . . . Oh, thank God!"

The last was delivered in heartfelt relief, for help had arrived in the shape of a stolidly reliable Aikins. "He . . . fell," she said helplessly, near to tears for some reason. "His bad leg—"

"I'm all right, Bob. But the damned fool got away. Baggett was right. I'm of little use to anybody anymore." The major sounded humiliated and immensely bitter.

Somehow Cat's place had been taken by Aikins, who said soothingly as he found the major's stick and helped him up, "Aye, they're slippery devils—the other one got away from Major Robinette as well. But no doubt you heard him lamenting the fact just a bit ago."

"Is everything all right?"

"As near as we can tell. The major was momentarily distracted and was jumped from behind. Chicklade got into the fight and gave a surprisingly good account of himself. But whoever it was managed to slip away when you let your popper off. No chance you grazed the fellow, is there?"

"I doubt it." Simon had come heavily to his feet and was

leaning on his stick, sounding, for the first time since she had known him, defeated and weary. "I was—"

"It was a miracle I wasn't killed," interjected Cat steadily, feeling his pain as her own. "It was only your quick reflexes that saved me."

He grimaced, but there was time for no more, for even at that moment a hoarse cry went up that heralded the worst nightmare of a stable. "*Fire!*"

After that, chaos reigned. The stableyard erupted with action, and it was only a miracle that there happened to be more men than usual present and that they had caught the fire so quickly. It had been set, obviously by one of the retiring invaders, in one of the nearest blocks; and though a stable, with its hay and wooden stalls, could go up quickly, they were able to put it out quickly enough with the help of the heavy fire buckets always kept ready by the stable well.

The real danger was to the horses, as the arsonist had undoubtedly known. All horses are terrified of fire, and if not blindfolded and led quickly to safety, can maim or destroy themselves in a mad frenzy against the walls of their boxes. High-strung racehorses are even worse. If they are not actually harmed by the fire or smoke itself, or manage to lame themselves trying to escape, the horror and excitement can go far toward making their chances in a race the next afternoon practically nil.

Cat had reacted instinctively at the cry, all other considerations having to be dropped for the moment. After what seemed several lifetimes, she and Jem Chicklade between them had managed to get all the horses out, while the others fought the fire itself. She had gone to Conqueror first, leading him out fairly quickly, the coat to her habit draped over his head. Jem had then shown her where Folly had been moved to a distant box earlier in the evening, out of harm's way.

As they worked, he managed to tell her what he knew of what had happened. Surprisingly, it had been at Lord Simon's insistence that a trap had been laid for Baggett's men—if that was who they had been. If an attempt was to be made on either of the horses, they had meant to catch the culprits in the act, using Lord Simon's horse as the bait and moving Folly safely out of danger. But unfortunately, Cat herself had unwittingly sprung the trap prematurely and allowed them to escape, setting the fire as they went.

Jem, stationed in one of the distant boxes to guard Folly, and feeling left out of the action, had abandoned his post without compunction when he heard the pistol shot. But by the time he had reached the stables, the fire had already been set. It was he who had raised the alarm.

After that, of course, there had been no time to think of capturing the escaping men. Jem seemed unnaturally stimulated by the night's events and lamented the fact long and loud. But Cat was scarcely listening. Once the fire was out and the danger past, she arched her back tiredly, her lungs still burning from the acrid smoke, and returned quickly to the now-smoldering yard.

The burned block lay black and forbidding, steam still issuing from its interior, while the cobbled yard was damp and full of puddles. After the heat of the fire and exertion, it was cold in the false dawn, and Cat suddenly shivered without her coat. She knew her hair was falling down and that her habit was streaked with smoke and soot, as was, undoubtedly, her face; but none of that mattered.

The firefighters were putting down their buckets, their faces and clothes blackened and singed by jumping sparks. In the increasing light Cat recognized Major Robinette, his cheerful grin showing white through his sooty face, and Chicklade, looking his age of a sudden.

Jamie was there too, for he had been roused from sleep

by the commotion and had thrown on his clothes haphazardly to help. He looked weary and a little stunned, but stimulated too, as Jem had. It was as if both had enjoyed the excitement.

Even Sir James was there, looking both angry and excited, with the disgraceful Patch at his side.

But Cat spared scarcely a glance for any of them, her eyes quickly passing on in search of the one blackened, exhausted face she was seeking. She had seen Lord Simon at several points earlier, propped incredibly against a wall and forming part of the fire brigade, his injured leg ignored or forgotten. Now she was grateful to locate him at last, still on his feet and sharing congratulations with the others.

During that long night he had not once glanced at her direction or seemed to remember her existence. Now, as she watched, Jamie came over shyly to thank him.

Simon smiled and made light of it, but even from a distance Cat could tell he was near the end of his strength. He was leaning very heavily on his stick, and had most of his weight off his weak leg. Underlying the soot on his face, his skin was almost gray with fatigue.

His friend must have recognized the fact as well, for Major Robinette came over to him then. He exchanged a few words with Jamie, but his eyes were watchful, and it was but a couple of minutes before Aikins, always highly protective of his master, was there with the major's curricle.

Simon hesitated, and glanced briefly round. But then he shrugged and allowed himself to be helped in. Major Robinette took the reins, and without another word they drove away.

Cat stood stunned, still paralyzed by that moment when she had seen the bitter defeat in Simon's face and had not known how to combat it. Since then her mind had raced agonizingly round and round, struggling with her own pride against the surprisingly strong need to wipe out forever that look of hurt and shame on his face.

It should not have mattered, for she had always known the end must come sooner rather than later. Tomorrow, when she refused his proposal, as she must, he would have walked out of her life anyway. This would merely spare her that one final painful confrontation.

But at the expense of his own pride, and she somehow could not allow that. The very fact that he had gone without looking for her told her all too clearly that he could not face her yet. And the importance of the race tomorrow, the attempt on the stables that night, the well-being of both horses—even her own future—all seemed to pale before that.

"Not this way," she whispered at last. *"At least don't let it end this way, in his bitterness and defeat."* It seemed to her in that moment that almost anything else would be preferable, including the trampling of her own pride if need be.

Suddenly nothing else mattered but that voice inside her head, urging her to action. She started, as if waking up from a deep trance, only to realize that the curricle had already disappeared.

Without realizing the decision had been made, she whirled and ran back toward the paddock where Folly was cropping grass after his disturbed night. She had no saddle or bridle, and he had to run a race he must win tomorrow, but none of that mattered either. The only thought in her mind was that she must catch Simon before it was too late.

What she was to say to him, especially in the company of two strangers, she had no idea. She only knew she had to see him tonight—wipe away that haunted expression from his face.

In an agony of impatience she managed to catch Folly, though after the terrifying night and her own obviously

unsettled state he was even more bad-tempered than usual.
He tried spiritedly to bite her, then objected to the
unaccustomed feel of her on his back without a saddle, but
she was in no mood for his temper, and he must have sensed
that. She grabbed a handful of mane and laid herself low
along his back and kicked him into a gallop.

She thought someone called her name as she jumped the
paddock fence and headed across the fields to save time, but
she ignored it, not daring to risk any delay. She did not know
why it was so important to her to catch Simon before he
reached Newmarket, or why whatever must be said couldn't
be said tomorrow just as well. She only knew that everything depended on her speed now, and despite the darkness
and the risks, she gave Folly his head.

As usual, Folly was not slow to catch her mood, and ran
like the wind. At any other time she would have enjoyed the
feeling of racing through the lessening night, the cool wind
in her face and the feel of that familiar, powerful body
beneath her.

Now she only cursed the delay, and urged Folly on ever
faster, beginning to fear that she had left it too late and had
already missed Simon.

When she finally reached the main road, she checked, her
heart sinking. There was still no sign of the curricle, and
it was obvious that she had indeed missed it.

She sat for a moment, knowing she should turn back. It
had been bad enough contemplating finding the words to say
in front of two others, but she could not face having to follow
Simon all the way into town, perhaps even the inn, and seek
him out there.

Then the memory of his face at that moment stiffened her
spine, and without another thought she turned Folly in the
direction of Newmarket.

Cat had at least hoped to overtake Simon along the road, but Major Robinette must really have been springing the chestnuts, for she still had caught no sight of them when she reached the outskirts of town. It was just first light, and Newmarket lay peaceful and still in the cool, misty morning.

Cat did not delay to admire the scene. She was half-afraid by now that she could somehow have missed them in the dark. But something drove her on, and so she rode boldly through town and into the inn yard.

There, she was at last rewarded by the sight of Simon's empty curricle, the chestnuts even at that moment being led away. The ostlers gaped at her, but she flung Folly's reins to one of them and sprang down without a word and went into the inn.

Afterward she was to picture with dismay what she must have looked like by then, her habit torn and filthy, her hair a mare's nest of tangles, riding bareback astride a lathered demon-black. At the moment she had no time to spare for her appearance.

The downstairs hall was mercifully empty, save for a chambermaid lighting the early-morning fire. She, too, gaped at Cat, but in answer to her snapped question at last managed to stammeringly reveal the location of Lord Simon Grey's room. But her eyes followed Cat's figure as she took the stairs two at a time, obviously sensing an intrigue.

Cat had already forgotten her, however. She climbed the stairs without giving herself time to think, and boldly knocked on Simon's bedchamber door.

She could vaguely hear voices inside, which halted at her knock. Then the door was opened to her by a disapproving stranger, obviously his lordship's valet. Even at that early hour he was dressed immaculately, as if he had been waiting up all night.

He seemed as surprised to see her as Cat was to see him, and instinctively half-shut the door. But she had caught sight of Simon by then, stretched on the bed, his face gray and his eyes closed, and she waited no more. She boldly stepped into the room.

Both Major Robinette and Aikins were bent over the major, hiding the lower half of his body from her view. She feared he had sustained more hurt than she knew, and her heart stopped, then lodged painfully in her throat. She had seen him on his feet only half an hour ago, so could not believe he was dead. But he looked so ill and exhausted that she was suddenly deathly afraid. She knew his wound was scarcely healed yet, and he had been pushing himself far too hard in the last weeks.

Then his voice, weary but sounding remarkably strong, freed her at last from her frozen position. "Damn you to hell, Jack!" it complained irritably. "I keep telling you I'm only bruised. And for your information, I've already endured enough heavy-handed mauling about in the last months without adding your efforts to the lot."

Major Robinette seemed to be making some inspection, but he retorted cheerfully, "Stop complaining, you ingrate! If you won't have the doctor sent for, you deserve our clumsy ministrations. Good God, I thought they sent you home to take life easy, you fool. Not mix with arsonists and horse thieves and beautiful Irish—"

His lordship's scandalized valet obviously thought it advisable to intervene, for he said hastily, "Er . . . ah . . . I beg your pardon, my lord. A . . . a lady is here to see you."

Cat had to endure the surprised stares of both Major Robinette and Aikins, as both quickly straightened. Not surprisingly, despite his near-disastrous *faux-pas*, Jack Robinette was the first to recover.

"Ah," he said, his eyes beginning to twinkle. "I fear I've

suddenly remembered something urgent I must attend to. And it requires the help of both of you. Be right back, old boy. Don't go anywhere without me. Miss Dunraven.''

He nodded to her as if the setting and hour were precisely ordinary, and then shepherded the two disapproving servants out of the room, leaving Cat, breathless and suddenly tongue-tied, to meet Simon's abruptly closed expression.

20

For a moment there was a long silence. Then he said quietly, "You shouldn't be here. I'll get Jack to escort you back."

She was suddenly self-consciously aware of her wet and bedraggled habit, her tangled hair and probably soot-stained face. He had been cleaned up, and lay, half-covered by quilts, his shirt open to show his strong chest with its covering of fair hair. The intimacy of the situation and the boldness of her actions in coming there suddenly nearly overcame her courage, and she closed her eyes, swaying a little in her own exhaustion. She had been mad to think he needed anything from her.

But at the continued silence, she at last opened her eyes again, and it was as if all her preconceived notions had been swept away. She saw that beneath his cool facade his face was gray and defeated, lines of weariness etched between his brows. There was no longer any sign of the charming and ever-cheerful Major Lord Simon Grey. He merely looked exhausted and in pain, and not the best of tempers.

She realized he must have looked like this for many long months before she had met him. Suddenly he was no longer the godlike figure she had foolishly always imagined him—the wealthy and handsome knight come to rescue her from herself. He was merely a man in need of love and comfort himself. She saw that she had been naive ever to imagine him any different.

With that realization, all notions of right or wrong, or of protecting her own pride, deserted her. Tomorrow would take care of itself, but now there was only this night—or rather morning—and perhaps there would never be another.

Her heart swelled with love, and something else, and she said simply, "I don't want to go back. How are you?"

He shrugged, turning his face away. "I've been better. Forgive me for not rising. But I think you had better go. You were right all the time. Tonight proved that."

'You saved my life tonight—not to mention the stables and both our horses."

He laughed bitterly. "Some help I was. When that devil had his hands on you, all I wanted . . . But instead, I was less than useless. Your friend Baggett was right—I am only half a man."

"I never thought to see you feeling sorry for yourself," she retorted. "I'm glad to see you are capable of such human emotions."

His eyes narrowed on her face, but at last he said with dangerous quiet, "What are you doing here, Cat?"

For a moment she couldn't answer. Then she began deliberately unfastening her damp habit jacket. "Exorcising a ghost," she said, and shrugged out of the jacket. "Or creating one."

There was a dangerous edge to his voice. "What's that supposed to mean?"

She sat on the bed beside him. "I thought I could walk away—disappear and never look back. But it seems I am more like my mother than I knew."

A little muscle began working in his lean cheek, but he

said nothing. Only when she next began to unbutton her soft lawn shirt did he put out an unsteady hand to stop her, his hand gripping hers rather harshly. "This has gone far enough. Do you think I want your pity, damn you?"

"Did you think I wanted yours? It seems pity is not the vile emotion I thought it. And love a harder trap to escape from than I hoped. Are you the only one allowed to be strong and giving?"

"Cat!" he said in a strangled voice. "You don't know what you're doing. You're overcome . . . exhausted . . . I don't know. But I can't let you—"

"You can't stop me," she said calmly. "Don't worry. I expect nothing from you. Nor have I any reputation to lose. I expect nothing but tonight. And I want that, not for you, but for myself, whether ghost or exorcism."

She evaded his hand and abruptly reached up to release the pins from her hair, shaking it so that it fell in midnight waves over her shoulders and back.

His chest was rising and falling rapidly now, as if he had been running, and she saw with satisfaction that some of the gray pallor had left his skin. "Cat . . ." As if against his will, his hand went up to the waves of her hair, then to gently touch the soft marks on her face. "That brute bruised you. When I saw you there, being manhandled, I . . ." His voice broke off, as if even now overcome with the thought.

Then it hardened. "But I had to accept tonight that I've been a fool to think my . . . handicap wouldn't matter. You deserve a man able to protect you—not prove a burden at the first sign of danger. You are so brave and strong yourself that—"

She silenced him by the simple expedient of placing her hand over his mouth, then leaned over to run her hands over his warm chest and press her lips to the pulse she saw beating there. "For a military man, you talk a deal of nonsense, Major Grey."

For a moment longer he resisted her. Then he groaned and swept her into his arms, completely ignoring his aching leg, and began to kiss her—her lips, her eyes, her face—as if he were starved for human contact. She, who knew that feeling far too well, let go of all her fears and insecurities and returned his kisses feverishly, with a hunger she had thought herself incapable of.

Her beating heart threatened to suffocate her, and she was glad when a t last he tore his mouth away, for she feared she might faint. "God, Cat! We must be sensible. But you go to my brain like the headiest Spanish wine."

"I don't feel very sensible," she said in a voice she scarcely recognized as her own. "I feel . . . I feel . . . Is it always like this?"

He laughed then. "No. This is very rare. Which is why I have to send you away before it's too late. Neither of us is in any shape to make rational decisions tonight, and if that weren't enough, I fear I'm scarcely at my best at the moment. Oh, *damn* this cursed leg!"

She roused herself to belatedly realize she was lying across him, no doubt causing agony to his already sorely tried leg. Guiltily she sprang up, and before he could guess her intention, had pulled the quilt away.

He made one convulsive attempt to stop her, then lay stiff and withdrawn and did not try to keep her from looking at his injured leg.

It was far worse than she had imagined, for the still new and ugly purplish scars crisscrossed his entire thigh, and the muscle was wasted and carved out, as if the ball had taken part of the leg with it. It was made worse by the new bruises from the night's activities that were already darkening around the scars. It was suddenly easy for her to see why the doctors had once despaired of saving the leg at all.

Her breath caught in her throat, and for a moment she felt almost physically ill, imagining what he must have been through, and the pain it must still cause him. She could only be glad that her falling hair hid her expression from his view.

But her silence must have betrayed her, for he said in an oddly harsh voice, "I warned you! I was a fool to think any woman could stand such a sight, especially one as beautiful as you are."

Suddenly her weakness no longer mattered in the face of his pain and his monumental misunderstanding. She raised her head so he could see the unaccustomed tears coursing down her cheeks, and whispered, "I never until this moment hated the French. But now I think I would volunteer myself if I could kill the ones who did this to you."

"Cat!" he groaned. "Oh, Cat."

In response she pressed her lips against the worst of the scars, anointing them with her tears. When he groaned again and tried to pull her up, she put her hand over his mouth to quiet him. "Hush, my love," she said unsteadily. "It doesn't matter. It will never matter again. If you could overlook my birth and my grandfather, did you really think I wouldn't be able to overlook so little a thing as this?"

When he pulled her up beside him, she was the one who drew his shirt from his shoulders and began to plant feverish kisses across his chest and neck and chin. She gave him no time for doubts, for there had been far too many doubts for both of them.

When he kissed her again, his mouth had ceased to be gentle, and if she had thought he had taught her all there was to know of passion, she was to learn very quickly how naive she was about the things that really mattered.

And certainly, if she had ever had any real doubts, he proved that Major Lord Simon Grey was indeed all man, despite his handicap.

It was he who finished unbuttoning her soft lawn shirt. When his hand, one surprisingly hard for a gentleman, pushed aside her shift and found her breast, she moaned aloud, genuinely frightened by the force of the emotions that shook her.

Instantly his hand stilled, and he said breathlessly, "Shh! Hush, my love. Cat . . . Caitlin . . . ! Oh, God, you're so beautiful. I should not. But I need you so much."

She had long ago realized that she could resist anger or violence, for it was what she was used to. But she had never had any defenses against his gentleness, and she should have known it from the beginning. He touched her as if she were something infinitely precious and fragile, to be adored and protected. And the time for all fear or regrets had obviously passed.

It was she who drew his head down to her, and when his lips replaced his hand she arched helplessly against him, with a wild, sweet longing that she only half-understood. She felt as if she had just discovered that all this time she had been only half of some whole she had never suspected until now, and without the other part of her she would never be fully alive.

Nor was Simon any longer the pleasant, easygoing man she had come to know. She had once or twice seen glimpses of his true identity, behind the mask of urbane gentleman he chose to wear. Once, as he had coolly faced down a man considerably larger than himself and unhampered by a nearly useless leg; and again tonight when he had betrayed no fear and ordered her captor to let her go.

But now she saw him perhaps as he was meant to be, loving

and ardent, gentle and sure. He swept her along with him as inexorably as the tide, confident and masterful, into waters that threatened to drown both of them. And if she still had no idea what tomorrow would bring, it was far too late for useless repinings. She had a lifetime of those behind her, and perhaps another lifetime ahead. But for tonight she would know love for once in her life.

Surprisingly, he was the one to call a halt at last, before they were both swept into the abyss. She herself was caught helplessly in the eddy, and would never have been able to save herself. In fact, she protested as he withdrew his mouth, and he held her tightly against him, gentling her and stroking her tumbled hair until she began to grow calmer, murmuring half under his breath, "Shh, my darling. It's all right. Hush, now, sweetheart."

But he was not as calm as he would have her believe, for she could feel the thundering beat of his heart beneath her ear, and the strong tremors that still shook his body and the arms that held her so tightly.

When at last she felt in some control of herself, she looked up, something like pain and bitter accusation in her eyes. "Why?" she managed shakily. "Why did you stop?"

His arms tightened a little. "Because, my darling," he said in a voice almost as unsteady as her own, "I refuse to make love to you for the first time when I am in pain and exhausted and you are overwrought and full of pity. Call it conceit, if you will, but I want your first experience with passion to be deliberate and beautiful, because you love me and for no other reason."

She raised herself on one elbow, her midnight hair streaming down to cover his chest. "Will you leave me no pride?" she demanded breathlessly. "Isn't it more than obvious that I love you? What chance did I ever have to with-stand you?''

He smiled, and tenderly smoothed her hair away from her face. ''I want neither to humble your pride nor to break your spirit, my beautiful thoroughbred Caitlin. When I take you, it will be as my wife, in the full panoply of law and church, and with everyone knowing it.''

She was shaken, and could not meet his eyes. But then his earlier words at last registered, and brought the familiar bitterness to her face. ''Are you so certain it will be my first taste of passion? You have little enough reason to think so, given my reputation and who my grandfather is.''

It was his turn to stop her mouth. ''I told you long since that I won't have anyone malign you, my sweet Cat, even you. Why does only your grandfather call you Caitlin, by the way?'' he added inconsequentially. ''I've always wondered.''

''I've seen no need to emphasize my Irish birth,'' she answered rather impatiently. ''But you haven't answered my question.''

''Haven't I? I like the name. It suits you. Caitlin.''

He smiled lazily at her and reached out to brush back a tumbled curl from her forehead, and she was almost undone again. She thought she would never again make the mistake of underestimating him, for at this moment he seemed to have completely sloughed off the mask of easy and well-bred amiability he often chose to wear. She thought this was how he must have looked the night before a battle: sure of himself, wholly unafraid, and lazily at his ease, inspiring his men to follow him anywhere as he gallantly risked his own neck time and again.

But she determinedly clung to her question. ''You haven't answered me.''

He looked faintly amused. "Then you force me to be blunt, my sweet. You are admittedly an apt pupil—in fact, I should have known from the fearless way you embrace the rest of life, that you . . . But I don't wish to put you to the blush, and quite frankly, at the moment my self-control is far too tenuous to risk getting into such dangerous waters again so soon, so we'll let it pass for now. But I am not without some experience, you know. Men can always recognize true innocence when they encounter it."

"Can they?" she inquired contemptuously, very much in her old style. "All men are fools if they think so. D'you think it's so difficult to counterfeit when necessary, then?"

He surprised her by throwing back his head and laughing aloud. "I admit it's been tried often enough. But I think you're willfully misunderstanding me. While I admit to a certain selfish pleasure in knowing I am the one who taught you to look like that, my sweet Caitlin, I would still want you had you had ten thousand lovers before me—including Baggett. Don't you know that yet?"

In the face of so much love and generosity, she felt oddly humbled. But a part of her dared not believe it, even yet. He was right. They had both been through a great deal, and now she had had time to think and rebuild her defenses. She felt like cursing him for stopping when he had, for she did not want to think tonight.

"You always know the right thing to say, don't you?" she inquired bitterly at last. "But you must know that I . . . have little experience with trust. I sometimes think it is a trick, like walking, that must be learned early, or not at all."

His face gentled, and he reached out to lift her face to him. "I know. It does little good to promise that I intend to make it up to you, my sweet, but believe me, I do. And now, I think Jack had better escort you home. It's only a few hours until the race, and though God knows I want you to stay, I care about your reputation, even if you don't. I don't want you to marry me because I have compromised you, but because you can't live without me—as I cannot live without you.''

She rose, unwilling to let him see that her eyes, which never cried, had misted over. But he would not let her get away with such subterfuge, or accept her sudden shyness. He insisted upon buttoning her shift and shirt, his eyes tender at her blushing—another thing she never did—and watched in fascination as she bundled up her hair.

As she was at last going, she stopped and said huskily, ''I haven't thanked you for what you did tonight.''

''And you're also not used to accepting help from anyone. I know that. But don't worry. We're even. I haven't yet thanked you for . . . what you did for me tonight. Don't worry about anything, my love. It will all be all right—I promise you.''

But in the cold light of dawn, as Cat rode wearily home, too spent even to be embarrassed by the tactfully silent Major Robinette's presence beside her, she was no longer so sure. Away from Simon's strength and the unexpected passion of his lovemaking, it was fatally easy to see all the obstacles still before them, and to know that no one human could promise another that. She might no longer see him as some fantasy figure, but as a man of flesh and blood, capable of pain and the need for love and reassurance, but there were still far too many things that could go wrong, and too much of a gulf between them. He might be able to overlook her birth, but she was still by no means certain she could.

She was suddenly unfairly angry with him for sending her away, for she might at least have had the memory to cling to. For she had told him the truth: she had too little experience with trust not to expect things to go wrong even yet. Hope was not an emotion she was much familiar with.

21

Even Sir James was subdued the next day, though nothing could quite quench his love of race day. It epitomized all he loved most in the sport—the feverish excitement, the outrageous wagers, the last-minute scratching of favorites, and the rubbing together of every type, from the nobility to the far more colorful tipsters, touts, jockeys, and trainers.

But if he could not quite hide his enthusiasm, no one else seemed to have caught the spirit of racing day. Few had gotten much sleep the night before, and they all knew that the night's disturbances had done little for either horse's chances. If Baggett's intention had been to burn them out so that Cat would have to marry him—or at the very least sell out to him—he had not succeeded. But with such high-strung animals he might have obtained his objective anyway, for there was now little chance that either horse would show well.

Cat tried to hide her worry, for horses were often more instinctual than people, but her lack of sleep, the night's events, and its aftermath all combined to nearly overcome her usual control.

As for the race, it had somehow assumed even more significance at a time when her chances of winning were lessened almost to nothing. No true gambler allowed himself to think of the consequences of losing, but she could think of little else. For so long what had loomed largest was the fear of losing the Downs, but that had now become an almost minor consideration. It paled by comparison with the decision facing her at the end of the day.

Simon had said he meant to claim her, whatever happened, and that could not help but appeal to the romantic in her. It was tempting to give up all decision and let herself be swept away, thus abdicating all responsibility for so difficult a choice.

But such feminine weakness had a habit of backfiring in the end, as her mother had learned to her cost. If Folly won, and she could go to Simon with her head held high, perhaps it would be possible. But he had not liked being the object of pity, and so should understand why she shrank from committing herself to a lifetime of playing the beggar maid.

At any rate, the fact that he had given her no choice would help her little when Simon grew tired of her, or ashamed, and began to regret so impetuous a gesture, for she had little doubt who would bear the brunt of the misery. And then there was the fact that she might effectively ruin him if she married him, for it was not beyond the realm of possibility that his friends, even his family, would cast him off were he to make such a misalliance.

If so, it were far better to marry Baggett and be done with it, for she did not think she could bear to see the love in Simon's eyes turn to contempt, or worse, or see him suffer the contempt of his friends for her sake.

Aye, far better. Baggett at least could never touch the real core of her being, or hurt her in the way Simon could, for she despised him already. But that was the problem, of course. Could she bear a lifetime of being pawed by him and being bullied and shamed by so brutish a husband? She was not the submissive fiber of which martyrs were made.

In short, the choice was impossible to make, a fat that had kept her tired brain whirling all morning. Marry Simon and run the risk of ruining him, or Baggett, and ensure her own misery. And she could not forget the fate of Sir James and Jamie, either. For though she had little doubt Simon would make a generous husband, it was perhaps asking too much to expect him to support a man he thoroughly disapproved of. At least with Baggett she would have the upper hand and could dictate terms of her surrender.

But for how long? Reality told her it would be only until he began to seek diversion elsewhere or tired of her aloofness. Then she knew she could count on very little but a lifetime of regret.

So whirled the questions, until her head was dizzy. Ruin herself or Sir James? Simon or all of them?

She was scarcely in a frame of mind to notice other people's problems, but Sir James's mood did not escape her. She had long suspected he was up to something, for he was never content with merely one arrow to his bow, and the disreputable Patch had been extremely busy the last few days. She would not put anything past him, and at any other time she would have been highly suspicious. But at the moment she hadn't the strength to deal with any new worries and so pushed it out of her mind.

Young Jem, who was to ride Folly, was also looking oddly jumpy, but she supposed she was doing the same. When she asked him if everything was all right, he evasively put his behavior down to having twisted his leg slightly the night before, fighting the fire. He assured her that he could still ride, however, and so she had to be content with his answer.

"It doesn't matter," she said. "I doubt that after last night he stands much of a chance—if he ever did. How does the betting stand?"

Jem flushed. "Much as you might expect. Rumor has it Baggett's money is on his ringer, and most seem to think he has the winning of the race with either. They say he has one hundred thousand guineas out. Da' says the field has been swelled by half-trained, half-broken horses sent to the post just to hold up the start, and that he's behind it. If so, it don't look good for either of our horses, for they're temperamental enough already."

He shook his head gloomily. "At any rate, word's got out about what happened last night, so Conqueror is holding at ten to one and Folly at twenty to one. You must know he's largely a joke."

Cat made herself shrug indifferently. "All the better if one of them wins." Jem and his father were to supervise the horses' journey to the track, and she added, "Take it slowly, and warn me if either shows any signs of not being able to race. I'll scratch both before I'll risk them unnecessarily."

Jem nodded, but then hesitated. "Beg your pardon, Miss Cat, but you aren't . . . backing Folly heavily yourself, are you?" he inquired anxiously.

"Good God, no. I can't afford to. What's Patch up to, by the way? Do you or your dad know?"

But Jem claimed ignorance, and she left it at that.

It was no surprise to her that Baggett was heavily backing his ringer against his own favorite. If she had had any money she would have been wise to do the same, for it seemed now that the race was a mere formality. With Folly seriously out of the running after the night before, she knew that no other horse could beat his Philanderer. If he was willing to pull his own horse, then the race would be no contest, and if he owned both the first- and second-place finishers, the race was unlikely to be protested.

It was diabolical, but she no longer much cared. She wondered where Simon was putting his money, then dismissed the subject from her mind as being too painful at the moment.

Jamie, Sir James, and Cat drove together to the racecourse well in time for the scheduled three-o'clock starting. Cat had not yet seen Simon that day, and was almost afraid to do so. She remained in the stable area until nearly starting time, wanting the race to be over and at the same time dreading it.

Both horses seemed to have endured the journey to the racetrack well enough. Nor did Folly seem to have suffered any obvious ill effects from his disturbed night and that wild ride into Newmarket afterward. But trainers usually allowed a horse to rest several days before a big race, so it had been unwise, to say the least, to risk him on such a ride. She and Chicklade went over him carefully, searching for any sign of swelling or tenderness in his feet or legs, but thankfully found none.

But then, if Jem were right and the field was being deliberately padded, Cat knew his chances were even further lessened, for he had yet to be tested in a race at all, let alone one where a clean start was clearly to be denied.

When Major Robinette wandered by, less than half an hour before the race was to begin, he was alone. Cat had had ample time to be embarrassed by her brazen behavior the night before, and could scarcely bring herself to meet his eyes, but he chatted easily of inconsequential topics and made no mention of having escorted her back from Newmarket at dawn that very day.

He apologized for Simon's absence, saying he would be along shortly, then looked over the horses with a knowledgeable eye and pronounced both remarkably fit after the excitement of the night before. Only as he was leaving did he add, with a grin, that he only regretted never having been privileged to see Miss Dunraven "witch" a horse, as Simon had informed him she could.

Dawn Lindsey

After he had wandered away, Cat was on the verge of leaving herself when she at last looked up to see Simon approaching. Only he was not alone. His father and brother were with him.

Cat's heart sank. She had seen both Salford and Denbigh at various times in her life before, but had never previously noticed the strong resemblance between them. All three, as they walked toward her, had the same indefinable air of elegance. But although the duke was distinguished and polite, his gray eyes were remarkably cold, and Lord Denbigh seemed to lack his younger brother's charm.

Then Cat had eyes only for Simon. His limp was more pronounced that day, particularly in contrast to his relatives' easy stroll, and she wondered how much pain he was in. But though he looked tired, it was impossible to read anything else in his face but polite interest as he bent his head to catch something his father was saying.

Despite all her warnings to herself to be sensible, for a moment Cat found herself irrationally hating both of his companions for their easy, graceful stride and calm assumption of good health, both of which made Simon's handicap seem all the more ugly and ungainly.

Then Simon laughed and put an arm affectionately around his brother's shoulders, and she saw that he was far more generous than she. It was obvious from that gesture that he was fond of his brother, at least, and had no thought of resenting him for his own obvious robust health.

She had it in her to wonder cynically if his attitude would already have changed toward her, in his family's presence. But he looked up then, and smiled at her, and not only did it do curious things to her pulse but also made her instantly ashamed of herself. Whatever else he was, Simon had made it abundantly clear that he was no snob.

He made the introductions as if suspecting no undercurrents, and the dreaded moment passed so easily in polite conversation that for a moment Cat was left feeling confused, wondering if Simon had told them anything about her. Certainly they seemed on excellent terms, for Denbigh was teasing his brother about his sudden passion for horse racing, and laughingly accusing him of having lamed the team he had lent him; and even his grace seemed interested in the bay's points and chances, asking intelligent questions and betraying no hidden motives or suspicions.

Then Cat found Salford's cold eyes on her as he listened to something his eldest son was saying, and all doubt died. They knew, then. And it was obvious that he, at least, did not approve.

She flushed despite herself, and looked away, only to find Simon's eyes also on her, with such a wealth of silent comfort in them that a little of her hurt was eased. A little, but not enough. She had her answer, it seemed. Despite his grace's suave good manners, she had no doubt that she had an enemy there.

Well, what had she expected? To be accepted with open arms? She did not know him well enough to guess whether he meant to actively oppose her, or whether he would ever go so far as to disinherit his youngest son completely if he made so shocking a marriage. But she would be a fool not to take the warning. There was respect and affection in Simon's attitude toward his father, and she should never risk coming between them.

Denbigh's attitude was harder to read, though he spoke more to his brother than he did to her. But she was glad when the warning was sounded and it was time for the weighing-in, for she thought she could not have endured much more of that polite but meaningless conversation.

The strained meeting had accomplished one thing, at least. She had her decision. The race now seemed almost an anticlimax.

22

Newmarket had not yet built a grandstand, one of the newfangled innovations in racing that Sir James so much deplored. Ladies were still a rarity on the course, and it remained a rough-and-tumble place, where drinking and carousing were as much a part of the day as racing, and where overenthusiastic and inebriated spectators continued to stray onto the course or gallop in with the finishing horses—to the imminent danger of both. The Jockey Club forbade but did nothing to prevent either practice, and more than one spectator had been trampled, or horse had to be destroyed as a result.

Before a race the field was always a bedlam of milling bystanders, wagerers, touts, and legs. The racehorses and their jockeys frequently got lost in the confusion, and nervous horses, such as Folly and Lord Simon's Conqueror, were at a distinct disadvantage. Nor was it unknown for a horse to be got at even there, before the start of the race. No one in that tangle would notice if someone strayed too close to one of the entries.

Cat had long deplored the practice, for that as well as other reasons. But even the building of rails had done little to keep the public off the course. Too many people like her grandfather resisted every attempt to codify the sport, and so changes, if they came at all, were perilously slow.

Another distinct disadvantage to any race was the starting. The present method was to have some man of considerable authority serve as starter, but in large fields such as today's, it was not unusual to have a dozen false starts and take more than an hour to get the field away.

Favorites could thus be deliberately impeded—and frequently were. Cat had seen races in which the obvious intention of the rest of the field was to deny the favorite a clean start. As soon as its jockey found a favorable position, it would be found that half the field was facing the wrong way. Nor was it unheard-of for even the starter to be in on the dodge, and deliberately delay the start until a particular horse was left many yards behind and blocked in by a contingent of half-broken and unmanageable horses.

Cat suspected something of the type would be tried today, for Baggett was known for such double-dealing. In racing, all one could do was be alert for any sign of trouble and try to avoid it.

Once the field was away, few of the spectators could tell one horse from another. This merely added to the confusion, and fights and even murders were not uncommon over disputes about which horse had actually won.

Cat had always disliked the actual race day, but it was not surprising that Sir James was in his element. The intrigue, the excitement, the skirting and subverting of the rules, the chance to pit his wits against others', were lifeblood to him. She sometimes thought that if he were on his deathbed he would revive sufficiently to take part in one last race day.

The Two Thousand Guineas was a relatively new race, but the audience was distinguished—and today included the newly appointed Prince Regent. Cat was not surprised to catch a glimpse of his portly figure standing in close conversation with the Duke of Salford, while a number of other noble gentlemen stood respectfully by. Nor should it have shocked her to see him laughing later with Simon, who looked relaxed and patently unawed by this condescension from his future sovereign.

But even so, it was another blow to the hopes Cat now saw as absurd. She had known who Simon was, of course, but he had been in her world, so to speak, and indeed had fitted in better than she would ever have imagined. But to see him suddenly restored to his own, rubbing elbows with the wealthiest and most important men in the kingdom, was like a dash of cold water in her face. Suddenly she was overcome by her brazen temerity in going to him last night, and could only be grateful he was kept away by the elevated company. She was not sure she could have dared to meet his eyes.

She had enough to occupy her thoughts anyway, for Sir James had disappeared shortly after they arrived, and she did not like to think what he was up to. His intuition had always been acute, but of late he had developed the habit of believing it infallible, and would back his instincts against incredible odds. Occasionally he still won, but he was as likely to pledge the Downs out from under them again on the back of some flashy nag with no staying power, or even Folly himself. When in the throes of his gambling fever, he seemed to have lost all control, and she was always justly nervous on race days.

But he owned both, when all was said and done, and there was nothing she could do if he chose to lose them. She could only shrug her slim shoulders and concentrate on those things she could control—which was precious little right now. Once race day arrived, a trainer's task was done and the jockey took over. And both were dependent upon the whim of an animal of steel muscle and nerves and something indefinable called heart. A horse who had it could win against incredible odds. One who didn't could show well in trial after trial and carry odds-on money, and still make a poor showing.

And even a horse with incredible heart could be defeated by such intangibles as the makeup of the field, the cleanness of the start, or deliberate interference by another jockey. And there was always the ever-present danger of injury. An animal that size thundering down the field on those incredibly slender legs, frightened and jostled by other equally excited horses, and surrounded by a frenzy of screaming and shouting spectators, could so easily take one fatal misstep. Cat had heard the sound too many times—and seen too many horses have to be destroyed—to ever mistake the delicate yet dreadful snapping sound of a leg being broken.

Jamie, as always, remained at her side, as much for protection as companionship; but neither had much to say. Too much depended on the outcome of the race, and both knew they stood little chance now, after the past night. Jamie looked as tired and drawn as Cat felt, and she spared a moment's empathy for him. His future hung in the balance fully as much as her own, for without the two thousand guineas' prize money, all hope of buying a pair of colors would have to be abandoned.

Then he caught her eyes on him and smiled gaily, pretending a cheerfulness she knew he did not feel. "Here they come," he said. "Poor Jem looks like he has the weight of the world on his shoulders."

Cat looked quickly to see young Jem Chicklade perched easily on Folly's shining back. She knew Folly could be dangerous, but Jem had ridden him enough to know how to handle him, and she had not thought him afraid. But the boy had been quite subdued for the last couple of days, in contrast to his usual cheerful unconcern.

She frowned, then was even more surprised to see Simon, away from his influential friends, standing at Jem's stirrups, apparently speaking earnestly to him. Jem's young head was bent down closely, but even as Cat watched, he looked up, his face oddly sullen, and walked Folly away.

That puzzled her, but even more disturbing was the glimpse she caught of Sir James standing in the ring, looking smugly self-satisfied. Cat followed the direction of his eyes and was in time to see the disreputable Patch sidling away from Baggett and slipping into the crowd.

She felt her heart lurch with an unnamed foreboding, but quickly looked away, unwilling to call Jamie's attention to it. And then there was no time for more, for the race was beginning.

She was not surprised to see Salford, the Prince Regent still at his side, serve as starter, for he was well-respected on the turf. And at least that meant they would be guaranteed a fair start, which was worth something.

Not much, however, for it quickly became apparent that word had gone out to deny a clean start. Time and again Salford would bring the horses up to the post, only to have things end in a tangle of plunging hooves and swearing jockeys, which meant it was all to be done over again.

Jem was doing his best to keep Folly out of it, but the confusion was having an inevitable effect on the black. Cat had always known that was a danger, for his hatred of other men and horses was so great that he could easily be driven to a frenzy. They had long ago decided to keep him back from the fray, even if it meant risking a poor start. Singly she was still convinced the black could outrun any of the horses in the field. The unknown was whether his desire to win could overcome his deep-seated hatred and fear.

Willis, on Conqueror, looked calm enough, and was doing a good job of keeping him up to the post. She had always liked and trusted him, and so could dismiss that worry, at least. Conqueror looked in prime health, and had shown no unpleasant repercussions from the disturbed night.

Chicklade joined them then where they stood by the rail, and Cat glanced at him. They were almost of a height, for she was tall for a woman and he short and spare. He met her eyes briefly, his expression bland, but Cat could sense the worry behind his eyes.

Then, after half a dozen false starts, without warning the field was away. Cat felt her pulse escalate with excitement and dread, and gripped the rail tightly; but she was too well-trained to reveal her tension in any other way. Folly was well back, but that was to the good. Jem was not to make his move untl the last quarter-mile, for once he gave Folly his head, he was unholdable.

Baggett's Philanderer took an early lead, but the ringer, Jerry, was some yards back from the post and got off to a slow start. The rest were in close conformation, and as the pack rounded the curve in front of them and thundered past, it was hard to distinguish one horse from another.

Then Cat picked out Conqueror, and her breath stopped. Willis was whipping him manfully, his face grim, but it was obvious the bay was dead meat. He was dropping back, his gait uneven and his sides already flecked with foam. Cat could have sworn he had not been gotten to, but whatever the cause—and it was doubtful they would ever know—he was already out of the race.

Cat's eyes unconsciously searched the crowd for Simon, the race forgotten. She dreaded to see the look of condemnation on his face, and though she knew she had done everything she could, she also knew she would have no defense against it. It was at times like these that she hated the sport most.

Her attention was at last recalled to the race by the roar of the crowd. Three furlongs from home, Philanderer was still several lengths in the lead, and those who had backed Jerry were beginning to howl with fury. Baggett's other entry was well back in the pack, and showed no signs of making his move.

It was time for Jem to edge Folly forward, and Cat's eyes strained to find the black, still hanging back. He was running well, showing no ill effects from the night before, but two other horses hedged him in. Jem, his face stark white, was hanging on grimly, but he seemed to be making no effort to get away.

Beside her she felt Chicklade stiffen, and a dark dread filled Cat's own mind. Folly was fighting to get through, but it seemed to her that Jem was deliberately holding him back. It was impossible to ride a race from the sidelines, of course, but she would have thought there was room enough on the inside to get by. Folly disliked running on the inside, but he seemed caught up enough in the excitement to temporarily forget this idiosyncrasy.

Jamie swore softly under his breath, and Cat knew it was not just her imagination. Instinctively her eyes went back to her grandfather's face, knowing the satisfaction she would find there. She felt sickened, and abruptly turned away.

Then another roar from the crowd, and Jamie's involuntary cry brought her back again. Two furlongs from home, she was in time to see Jerry make his move. Philanderer still clung to his lead, but to her experienced eyes it was obvious that he was being subtly pulled as Jerry surged forward. The rest of the pack was falling behind, and Cat now had no doubt how the race would end—how it had been meant to end from the beginning.

Her eyes again sought out Folly, and she was not surprised to see he had fallen even farther back. She could sense Jamie's puzzlement and Chicklade's tension, and could not bear to look at either. She felt intensely sorry for Chicklade, who had been almost like a father to her, and was suddenly furious—not at Jem, but at the whole world of the turf, which put too much emphasis on something as unimportant as a horse race.

Worse, she knew heself to be as guilty as anyone, for despite her dislike of that element of the sport, she had staked everything on the outcome of one race—her own and Jamie's future, possession of the Downs, everything. It suddenly seemed absurd and unreal that fortunes could be won or lost, reputations made or broken, the lives of horses and humans risked on so childish an event.

Then she felt a calm hand on her shoulder, and did not have to look back to know who had come to stand quietly behind her. She looked up at him, the race forgotten, and said foolishly, "I'm sorry!"

He bent his head close to hear her words in the noise that surrounded him, and his eyes were full of compassion. "Why should you be sorry?"

"Conqueror. I should have . . . I don't know what. Something! It's obvious Baggett got to him. I know you wanted to make an impression in front of your father and brother."

He laughed easily, and she saw then that he was above needing to prove something to anyone, even his august relations. "That doesn't matter. It's you I'm worried about."

But she sensed a tension in him to match her own, as of a fine wire held taut. He was looking over her head, watching the race still, frowning a little, as if waiting for something, though his horse stood no chance of winning now. She could no longer bear to look, however, and so stood foolishly waiting, every sense dulled.

Then unexpectedly something flared in Simon's eyes and he turned her abruptly back to face the track, as if he had every right to touch her in public. "Look!" he said softly.

For a moment she was too conscious of his hands on her shoulders to be able to focus again on the race. As she had expected, Philanderer had fallen back and Jerry was edging past, to the mingled excitement and fury of the crowd. Then Cat stilled as she saw another familiar head break forward, straining even with the other two.

Jamie was almost beside himself, and even Chicklade had so far forgotten himself as to pound the railing in his excitement. Cat feared it was too late, and wondered why the fact didn't mean more to her than it did.

Then Folly's black head crept past as the finish line flashed by, and the crowd erupted. Jamie swung Cat off her feet, whirling her around and around, and Chicklade was slapping Lord Simon's back, all social class forgotten. Cat was breathless when Jamie let her go to throw his arms around Chicklade. Then they were surrounded by friends and well-wishers.

Cat wondered why she felt nothing—no elation, no relief, nothing. She wanted only to escape, and her eyes searched frantically for Simon, who had been separated from her in the crowd.

Then he was miraculously beside her, and seemed to sense her need, for his arms protected her from the crush and got her somehow safely outside the crowd in a little oasis of calm.

She remembered his leg then, for she had been jostled and bruised. But he betrayed no pain. Only his eyes seemed watchful and waiting.

"Well?" he said quietly. "Your reputation as a trainer is made. You should be proud of yourself."

She shrugged cynically. "For the moment. The turf has a very short memory."

"But you've won. You can be independent now. Isn't that what you've always wanted?"

Aye, she had won. She had trouble keeping the bitterness out of her voice. "Until Sir James risks it all again—if he hasn't already." Then she met his gaze directly. "You know, don't you?" she demanded. "Was it Sir James?"

Then she closed her eyes against the compassion in his own. "I knew he was up to something. He asked Jem to hold Folly back, didn't he?"

"Don't be too hard on him. He thought Folly stood no chance—especially after last night. At any rate, he's been punished enough, for he backed Jerry heavily, I suspect. And don't blame Jem either. He thought he was doing it for you too, and even so, it was tearing him apart."

She thought how peculiar it was that he should be defending her grandfather to her. "How did you know?" she asked at last.

He shrugged. "When you have as much experience with young men as I have, it wasn't very hard. I thought Jem had been looking hangdog for some time now, and after last night, I persuaded him to confide in me."

She laughed bitterly. "I thought I was protecting you, and instead I'm the one who was naive. I feel a complete fool. I didn't even see what was before my very eyes."

But he refused to be sidetracked any longer. "All of this is beside the point. You know what I'm waiting for," he pointed out steadily.

She looked up at him then, and there was no more room for subterfuge between them. "I know," she whispered. "I thought I knew what my answer was—must be!—but now it seems I'm certain of nothing anymore.''

''You don't know how promising that sounds, sweetheart. You know I said I would take you no matter what.'' He sounded uncharacteristically stern.

She waited breathlessly, longing to have the decision taken out of her hands. She had meant to be strong, but now she discovered she was not strong where he was concerned—she was every bit as weak as her mother had been.

''But I've discovered I was mistaken.'' He spoke gently, as if to ease the hurt of his words.

Her eyes flew to his, and her heart threatened to deafen her with its pounding. ''I . . . I see.''

''No, I don't think you do. I want you to come to me of your own free will. I learned belatedly last night how important pride can be. I would never rob you of yours. You don't need me. You can pay off your debt to Baggett.''

She wondered how he knew of it, but it didn't seem to matter. ''Aye—and I've a grandfather who could betray even his own horse if the price were great enough!''

''Then this should help.''

He handed her a slip of paper. Wonderingly she unfolded it, to discover it was a five-hundred-guinea bet on Folly to win.

She began to tremble. ''You . . . you backed Folly? You . . . When even my own grandfather doubted him?''

''You believed in him,'' he said simply. ''That was enough for me.'' Then he grinned. ''At any rate, you may not thank me when you discover that this was your fee for training Conqueror. Had Folly lost . . .''

He shrugged and didn't finish the sentence, but it didn't matter. Nor did his quiet addition, ''You're a rich woman

now, in your own right. You have no need to marry me if
you don't want to.''

The enormity of his gesture—and its delicacy—over-
whelmed her. He had given her back her pride, but somehow,
in the process, she seemed to have no need of it any longer.
"I . . . I . . . Are you *sure?*" she asked foolishly.

Then she was in his arms, and it didn't matter who had
made the first step or that they were standing in the middle
of a crowded racetrack. Nor did it matter that he had had
to drop his stick to receive her, and stood in imminent peril
of falling without her support.

Certainly neither of them cared at that moment that Folly
had just won the Two Thousand Guineas and the crowd was
no doubt waiting for her to appear with him in the winner's
circle.

But as Simon continued to kiss her, they were finally
reluctantly startled apart by Sir James. "It's about time,"
he remarked blandly. "I was beginning to think my plan
would be ruined by my own granddaughter's stubbornness."

Cat pulled back immediately to say wrathfully, "*Your*
plan? Why, you . . .''

He looked offended. "Aye, my plan. I hope ye don't mean
to deny it was me who brought his lordship here in the first
place. Ye didn't think it was an accident, did you?"

"I think you brought him here to fleece him!" retorted Cat.

"It's little enough faith ye have in me, Caity," he said
mournfully. "I hope his lordship here will teach ye a little
trust.''

Cat was still glaring at her grandfather, but Simon put out
a hand to her, his smile incredibly warm. "I hope I will.
As for you, sir, I must confess at this point I wouldn't put
anything past you—even planning this from the beginning.''

He held out his hand to his future grandfather-in-law. "But

whether or not you planned it, I'm forever in your debt, for your granddaughter is the only woman in the world for me. I hope I have your permission to marry her, but I warn you that I mean to marry her whether I do or not.''

Sir James shook his hand readily. "Aye, aye, I'm resigned to it. But there's settlements and the like to be considered first. I'll not have my Caity going penniless to ye.''

"Grandfather!" Cat said warningly.

He ignored her. "But that can all be tended to later. What I'd really like to talk to you about is a little joint venture, me boy.''

"*Grandfather!*"

"My Caity has racin' in her blood, ye know. This afternoon has proved that. She may even rival me one day. And ye've long had the ambition to rival your father, no doubt. What I thought was, we could expand the Downs, use Folly at stud to sire a new race of champions and—''

"Grandfather. No.''

At her flat voice, Sir James and Simon turned to look at Cat, a question in both their eyes.

"No? After today ye can say that, girl?" demanded her grandfather.

"It's all right, sweetheart," Simon said quickly. "I know you love the sport.''

"No," she said again. "I don't mind managing my husband's stables, and I will always love horses, but I want to get as far away from Newmarket and the turf as possible. And Jamie will have his pair of colors. You own the Downs free and clear again, Grandfather, but I want nothing more to do with it.''

"Are you sure, Cat?" Simon asked her.

"I have never been so sure about anything in my life before." She smiled at him and added softly, "Except that I love you.''

"Ah, well," Sir James said philosophically. "It's a hard girl ye are, Caity-lass."

But as Lord Simon hugged her to him and they began walking toward the winner's circle, Sir James stationed himself on Simon's other side and added for his ear alone, "But if ye were in the market for a sure thing, me boy, I can promise you . . ."

Simon grinned and tightened his arm about Cat.

SIGNET REGENCY ROMANCE
COMING IN JANUARY 1990

---•---

Dorothy Mack
The Reluctant Heart

Elizabeth Hewitt
A Private Understanding

Irene Saunders
The Doctor's Lady

---•---